Backlash of
Mono Fulfillment

Fish Tales with the Captain

Captain Brian E. Smith

Published by:
Southern Yellow Pine (SYP) Publishing
4351 Natural Bridge Rd.
Tallahassee, FL 32305

www.syppublishing.com

This is a work of fiction. Names, characters, places, and events that occur either are the products of the author's imagination or are used fictitiously. Any resemblance to actual persons, places, or events is purely coincidental.

The contents and opinions expressed in this book do not necessarily reflect the views and opinions of Southern Yellow Pine Publishing, nor does the mention of brands or trade names constitute endorsement.

ISBN-10: Trade Paperback 1-940869-68-4
ISBN-13: Trade Paperback 978-1-940869-68-1
ISBN-13: ePub 978-1-940869-69-8
Library of Congress Control Number: 2016931647

Printed in the United States of America
First Edition January 2016

Contents

Foreword
Donn Shilling

If you want the "experience of your life time" go fishing with Brian Smith. Your trip will be like going on an adventure with your best friend. And when it's over, you'll want to go again. The experience is such because Brian Smith loves life and fishing—and his wife, friends and family.

We first met when I was young—not much older than then Brian. He was thin and quiet and ready to begin the next phase of his life. He had just finished two years in the Peace Corps, helping farmers in Honduras increase food production. Like him, I was just beginning my career and full of life, passion, enthusiasm, and naiveté. All good traits—but unknown to me at the time was Brian's true passion—fishing, or at least the process and camaraderie, if not the actual act of catching fish. Anyway, at our first meeting (I was an Assistant Professor at the University of Florida and Brian was interested in pursuing a Master of Science degree with me), I was immediately struck by Brian's energy and interest in doing something of value for mankind. We discussed my program, graduate school, various types of research projects and of course life in general. At the time, he did not discuss fishing. To get my students adjusted to graduate school, I provide them with "a plan," which includes assigning office space, course work, a request to develop a research plan and an assigned project. He got off to a quick start. Everyone, including me, liked Brian. He was always willing to help out with work and was always ready to have some fun. My group worked and played together. It turns out that Brian is quite the athlete.

We played softball, basketball, golf and tennis—fishing came later for me, although I think Brian started fishing in the Gulf of Mexico from day one. Brian could hit a golf ball a mile with what seemed to be no effort. When we played tennis he would basically stand in one spot and hit the ball to alternating corners of my side of the court. I would run myself ragged unable to keep up. I guess this would not have been so embarrassing except Brian at this point of his life was a very "big boy" and seemed to always wear combat boots to the tennis court. He would inevitably slow the pace so as to avoid either killing, pissing-off, or embarrassing his major professor. This turned out to be a recurring theme of our relationship. I remember fishing at Crescent Beach (50 miles south of Jacksonville). This trip turned out to be one of many memorable cavorts. We of course stayed up all night, caught fish, and more to my point, I provided Brian with one of numerous opportunities to kill, piss-off and/or embarrass me. Early on the morning of the second day of this trip I asked Brian to teach me to use a cast net. After extensive training (ha ha), I took the cast net and tried to execute a full speed throw—not a good idea. The next thing I knew Brian was over top of me with my head in his hand shaking me. It turns out I didn't release the bottom part of the net at the appropriate time so about 1 pound of weight (the bottom of the 8 foot radius net has about 16 one oz. weights distributed evenly around the edge) had rapidly rapped around my head and knocked me out cold. When I came to, the concerned look on Brian face was one I would see again. So was his next reaction which consisted of uncontrollable laughter. As would often be the case, I joined in.

A colleague of mind once asked me how Brian was doing. I told him great. He conveyed a surprised look with a smirk so I asked…why the smile. He said he frequently saw Brian heading to the gulf coast early in the morning during the work week. I asked how he happened to see Brian so frequently. It turns out he lived on the road between Gainesville (home of UF) and Cedar Key (small town of 1000 on the coast of the Gulf). After a brief discussion, with Brian I found myself invited on my first fishing trip. I had done a limited amount of fresh and salt water fishing, but over the next several years I learned what fishing was really about. Our rendezvous was early in the morning at

Brian's apartment. I was attempting to keep this trip clandestine. I was trying to avoid anyone knowing that I/we were going fishing; especially my colleague. Brian had a 14 ft. skiff with a 20 hp motor—very used. After provisioning, we headed to the water. Before we reached the sprawling metropolis of Cedar Key, we turned off on a back road paved with oyster shells. We wound around for about 2 miles before we arrived at our launching site. What an incredible view. I felt like I had been transported back hundreds of years. No evidence of civilization. This area of Florida is very remote—mostly pine forests and mangroves dotted small islands and oyster bars. The water depth is very shallow. Successful launching and landing can be tide dependent. Shortly after setting out, Brian provided me with a light tackle rig, a weighted hook with a plastic grub. Within in minutes I had hooked a 2 lb. Jack Cervalle. I was still catching fish when Brian informed me that we were leaving what to me was the best fishing spot ever—little did I know what was in store for the rest of the day. It was about 8 am as we continued to motor out through narrow tidal channels. I continued to fish and caught speckled trout and red fish. More diversity and numbers of fish then I ever dreamed possible. Once we reached the open gulf Brain asked me to retrieve my line and sit. We headed to one of the small islands and anchored. Brian had a very small rod and reel rigged with about 6, very small gold hooks, with a ¼ oz. weight at the end. He lowered to line into the water and within seconds brought in 2 or 3 Pin Fish which he put in his version of a live-well--basin with water but no circulation. Graduate student don't have much money. After catching about 2 dozen pin fish, we hoisted the anchor and moved to what seem to be uninteresting open water. Boy was I uninformed. As we slowed, I noticed a floating plastic milk jug. Then I saw several others. Brian had meticulously surveyed this area by methodically ascertaining the location of deep water channels visually (probably 10 -12 ft. verses the generally flat 3-6 ft. bottom). He then baited a heavy rig with a pin fish and tied a balloon about 10 ft. from the hook. We then drifted, waiting for a strike. I still can't believe what happened. After catching several small (2 to 10 lbs. – huge to me until I fished with Brian) fish (shark and gar) the free spool began to "sing" and the balloon moved rapidly across the water before disappearing. Brian grabbed the rod and began

3

an epic battle with what would turn out to be a huge fish. After about 40 minutes, Brian reached into the water and hosted what must have been a 10 ft. 150 plus lb. Tarpon. The fish was bigger than Brian, me, and the boat. We of course had no camera and had to release the fish. We did keep one scale—about as big as your hand—as evidence of the incredible catch. I think it was still just before noon and I had experience what would turn out to be the best day of fishing ever. Clouds were on the horizon, and we had already experienced more fishing then any person was entitled to so we headed in for lunch which included food, cold beverages and billiards (no surprise, Brian is also an excellent pool player). The good news was we would have many more unbelievably great days of fishing, but none would top my first day fishing with Brian.

I could go on and on as we had many memorable days of fishing. I truly miss our times on the water. This brief period of my life has and will continue to be cherished. Let me end with… if you want a, "Never to be forgotten" life experience that includes incredible fishing, contact Captain Brian. In the meantime, it turns out that in addition to all the other things Brian loves he is a great writer as you are about to find out. Although fishing with Brian is more fun than reading about fishing with Brian, you will enjoy his second book; I did.

Introduction

I have had this ailment for as far back as memory allows. Mom told me my Uncle Tom was the one who gave it to me when I was a mere toddler. At the time, Dad was in Korea, serving in the Army. Mom and I were living with Mawmaw, my grandmother, in Montgomery, West "by God" Virginia. My Uncle Tom lived in nearby Kimberly holler and was around me a lot. He was stricken by the same ailment all his life and had to be the carrier. At my young age, I was vulnerable, yet the weird thing was that not one of my kinfolk tried to protect me from picking up Uncle Tom's affliction. I actually overheard them say, "If it doesn't kill 'em, it'll make 'em stronger."

The progression of my disorder was recently published in a three–hundred page manuscript. Strangely, the disorder had never been named. I asked, "What is wrong with me?" I'm fifty-two years old now, and what started out as an occasional itch has now taken over my life. It has developed in to a full-blown degenerative career. I named my problem "Mono-fulfillment" for which I hope there is never a cure.

This book is a follow-up to my first about growing up, fishing. However, at this point, things have become critical. I've gone professional…fifteen years as a charter captain. I write the following collection of stories from my helm. I've had the privilege of greeting and getting to know many amazing and wonderful folk (99.92%), as well as an insignificant number of others, usually with greater than 0.08% blood alcohol content by volume, and very few naturally insufferable people. I disregard the very few encountered idiots because children have literally grown-up, gone to college and/or made careers, got married, and returned with their new spouses and children over the summers. I don't feel like I have aged; obviously I have. Now I have to look up to talk to young men or eye-to-eye with young women I used to kneel down by to help catch a fish.

Occasional pains in my arms, knees, and back remind me as well that time waits on no man. I believe time served in poor sea conditions is an age accelerant. A bad sea is undefeatable; a good boat is durable, but the body is prone to give way over time. Yet, I am at peace with it all. I always look forward to my next fishing adventure with friends I've known and new friends I've yet to meet.

The following is a collection of short stories I've had the joy of living. They run the gamut from small fish to huge fish, kids to grand parents, friends becoming more like family, turtles to radios, conservation to misbehavior, and this and that. My wish is that the stories take you back to a place or time in your life you thoroughly enjoyed and remember fondly, or that they take you on a new adventure with me at the helm. Either way, I thank you for spending your valuable time with my writings and hope the fish tails are pleasurable reading.

Sincerely, Capt. B

No life is so happy and so pleasant as the life of a well-govern'd angler.
Izaak Walton

Have Some Fun

It was a fine Saturday in May in Steinhatchee, Florida. The weather forecast was a pleasant, refreshingly cool morning temperature, followed by a comfortably warm but not hot daytime high temperature. Added to this were pleasant sky conditions of background blue, dotted with cotton-ball clouds and no chance of rain. There was a light wind, 5-10 mph, from the southwest. Sea forecast was two foot or less. It was a fishing prescription I wish I had the authority to write for every charter.

Garrett, my mate, and I, mostly Garrett, prepped the boat. Garrett had been working with me for over a year on weekends during school and through one summer. He was now a senior in high school and knew exactly how to setup the boat for a charter.

My wife, Gina, pushed us together when I found myself in need of a mate. "This young man in my Sunday School class would make a great mate."

My initial opinion, "Sissy, scrawny, afraid to get fish nasty and bleed doing so, prone to sea-sickness, chalky lightweight who would embarrass me the first trip offshore and get shocked by some of the language some men use on the boat." I was wrong about Garrett, meaning my wife was right and still reminds me at every opportunity.

At sixteen, he was big enough to wrestle a feral pig to the ground; ironically, now he enjoys doing just that. Anyway, he was smart, reliable, loved the sport, and knew much about fishing. Most importantly, he had a personality that worked well with people from anywhere. He and I gelled like peas and carrots.

Our guests on that charter were a family. The father was David, an electrical engineer working in and out of Atlanta. His wife, he introduced to me as Poot. Their young son, Davy, was still small and lightweight—sixty pounds—enough to require a life-vest when motor's running.

The morning meet-and-greet was hurried along by the incessant nagging nips of our resident sand gnats, locally called "no-see-ums." We were away from the dock in a "no see-um" feeding rush. Davy was placed between Poot and me on the captain's bench. He was suited up in his bright "fishing vest," legs sticking straight-out, too short to be able to hang down over the seat edge.

Davy couldn't see much from his vantage point, but what he did observe, he made questions of during our idle period.

"Mister Captain, what is that long thingy that looks like a snake?"

"That is a rubber eel, a lure I use to catch a fish called a cobia that can get longer than you are tall."

"Is that a TV?"

"Actually, that is a machine that lets me see the bottom of the ocean; it's called sonar."

"Why do I hear people talking?"

"That is a radio that allows fishermen to speak back and forth to one another."

He ended his question salvo with "Do you know what you're doing?"

"Give me a break Davy; it's my first week on the job, and I'm still trying to figure things out myself." Poot snort laughed.

As we passed by the end of the no wake zone, Davy asked, "What are we going to do today?"

I said enthusiastically, "We're going to have some fun!" I opened up the throttles as well as Davy's eyes toward the awaiting, happy wide-open. *"Yes we are,"* I said silently to myself with the sun likewise opening up beautifully behind us.

The joy is in the journey.

Fishing Wasn't Such an Imposition

The story title mimics a lyric from the song, "Live Like You Were Dying." It's a heartfelt tune sung by Tim McGraw, written by Tim Nichois that instantly became popular as it plucked the heartstrings of many—those dealing with the topic personally and/or everyone else who had, is, or will deal with it in regards to themselves or a loved one. A grave illness brings drastic changes to all in our odd-shaped circle of life. What was real important, such as career, a step up the corporate ladder, school, sports, hobbies, a planned retirement, or anything else, fades to a narrow, one issue focus. Life jumbles; our perspective is replaced.

Recently, I met a variety of people who were going through the wringer of life. Each had a different problem but suffered the same. I know everyone who reads this story can relate in some way. No one is immune.

It made me think about how trivial my aggravation over asinine fishing regulations was. The epiphany came after I went through the spiel of what fishery was open, what was closed, and when some were going to be re-opened.

Then a lady said, "We just need to have some fun." Her eyes were weary, showing the emotional and physical drain of what was going on in her life.

I said, "Yes Ma'am," feeling more than her words.

The next half hour was spent catching pinfish. Within five minutes, she was engrossed in catching bream-sized, live bait. She looked like a woman without a care in the world. *Wow*, I thought!

During the forty-five minute ride offshore, I thought about it more. I came to a simple conclusion: Recreational fishing is supposed to be fun by the definition of recreation. She and the rest needed fun…, and a bunch of it.

We came to rest over a piece of hard bottom that held a bunch of Florida snapper. Light action gear put more fun in the mayhem. During the hour of catching, I watched a silly wiggling fish, any fish, temporarily take people away from their problems.

A prolonged stop at an amberjack hole shot the moon as the action was nonstop. We ended up throwing hookless plugs into the mass of fish just to watch the fish crash into one another while going for the plug. We picked up some grouper and a small kingfish during the course of the day as well.

Everyone was happy when we returned to the dock. Some important matters had been momentarily forgotten. Saying goodbye, she smiled and hugged me. Her eyes reflected the rejuvenation of her soul. I wished I could put that time in a bottle and give it to her so she could have a medical swig of joy and love when she really needed it most.

Love is a symbol of eternity. It wipes out all sense of time, destroying all memory of a beginning and all fear of an end.
Madame de Stati

Pinfish

During the red tide, I couldn't find a pinfish, at least one that wasn't floating. Those little pinfish—saltwater breams we catch for bait so quickly and easily and take for granted—are the simple bases that put smiles on faces. It is nigh impossible for any saltwater predator to resist the sashay wiggle of a happy, healthy pinfish. Any seasoned, saltwater angler's confidence meter is pegged on high when a pinfish is pegged on his hook.

When drift fishing the flats, I use a hefty spin combo to set back a pinfish tethered under a large cork in hopes of a surprise cobia—or anything else considerable—taking me from behind while jigging for trout on the leeward side. One trip, I had an oversized pinfish under a cork. It dragged behind for quite a while. I heard a commotion and turned to see a gator trout wallowing on top, trying to eat the pinfish. I had to watch and wait for that gator trout to manage to fit that pinfish in its mouth. It seemed forever before the cork finally went down the hatch. I thought the deal was done and snatched. I snatched the pinfish from the trout's mouth…, I believe to the relief of both.

Follow me here; I remember flipping a corked pinfish to the edge of some rock grass while fishing the flats. You don't have to be a botanist to recognize rock grass. It grows on lime-rock—think name association. BB-sized, gas-filled, plant bladders, amongst the leaves, float the unrooted part of the plant above the bottom. Plant growth continues till it tops out on the surface. From that stage, it begins spreading horizontally, forming a shady mat on the surface. Redfish are fond of rock grass habitat like a fat man suspended in a hammock under the shade of two old, live oak trees with a cooler of cold beer within arm's reach. Seeing rock grass is good fisherman information.

Once splashed down, the hooked pinfish dipped and dragged my cork around, behaving as an undersized, under-trained boxer knowing he was going to be KO'd moments into round one. The pinfish was spot on.

A V wake rocketed out from the rock grass, inhaling the hapless "pin-boxer." The bright, yellow cork shot back into the rock grass jungle. I set the hook to feel a strong wobble. The fish shot from under the rock grass canopy with the bright, yellow cork chasing it like a tracer bullet across the gin-clear water of the flat. The fish pressed my fishing skills. I had to apply a touch and go finger drag on the spinning reel spool. I got another education as well as a challenge. The redfish had twelve spots and was over-sized, twenty-nine inches.

Over time, that little pinfish cost thousands of dollars and wifely arguments because the memory prompted countless fishing trips to try and recreate the single event as many times as possible.

***

Now let's go to the big docks where the multiple-day, offshore party boats depart for the Florida Middle Grounds. There are marvelous redneck-engineered achievements made to sustain a personal batch of pinfish for the long trip. That "Cracker *MacGyver*" will lug a seventy-pound, homemade pinfish accommodation a hundred yards to the boat at four am. Ironically, he can't stand to tote groceries in from the garage for his wife.

Why all the extra effort for a pinfish? Just to have the opportunity to feel a pinfish freaking-out at the end of the line when a grouper, red snapper, or whatever is enticed to accept the sacrificial, live offering at the rock alter below.

I wish I could vote one of those, pinfish *MacGyvers* into the White House. This little "pinfish" would feel comfortable, knowing my "life-well" was built and protected by someone with proven, common sense, and especially if there was a sensible budget involved beforehand. That *MacGyver* would spur an American revitalization. But no soapbox; this is about pinfish.

Coming to rest near an Air Force tower, over a wreck or any other haunt, and seeing a big wave of large amberjack greet the boat just below the surface, makes me feel somewhat sorry for the pinfish swimming around in the livewell. I'm no bunny hugger, but the pinfish doesn't have a chance of making it out alive once picked from the confines of its re-circulating boat jail.

The water was clear. We could all see the horde of amberjacks rushing up around the boat. We watched as the free-lined pinfish splashed down. The stress-free swim lasted for the first second or two. Its newfound freedom quickly turned to terror. Once refocused, its life was "more gooder" in the re-circulating boat jail. Seeing the overwhelming menace below and incoming quickly, it dashed away toward the surface, hoping to sprout wings in the next few seconds and fly away from the danger. No wings developed, just a frantic, yard-long dart at the surface before it was boiled gone and someone yelled "Fish On." And the amberjack kept boiling on until we released all our prisoners from boat-jail.

During another charter someone said, "Look at that shark." I glanced that way to see a four-and-a-half to five-foot, brown fish lollygagging off the starboard side. It's not a shark. It's a cobia. It's a cobia! I start shaking like Barney Fife trying to get his bullet from his shirt pocket. I vibrated back to the cutting board, grabbed two handfuls of whatever bait happened to be there and tossed it towards the fish. My action was to chum the waters, thereby enticing the cobia to linger around long enough for me to present a pinfish.

In my youth and as a young man, I pitched baseball, was a starting guard in basketball, and played tennis for high school and college. But in that state of crazy, I tossed the chum at the fish with all the natural grace of a very effeminate gay man throwing a football for the first time. Some chum made the water, some stayed in the boat, and some stuck to the two guys standing on the starboard side.

"Sorry, now get out of the way," I said, after grabbing a large spinning combination spooled with fifty-pound braid, with a three foot section of sixty-pound, fluorocarbon leader and a hook tied on the end. I was simultaneously trying to smoothly shake a pinfish on the hook. After two punctures to the thumb marked in blood, the pinfish was on the hook, and I rushed the starboard rail. People willfully and promptly stepped away from the captain who appeared, from all outward behavior, to have completely lost his mind. Their self-preservation kicked in without questions.

While I was losing it, the cobia was mulling around the chum that made it in the water. Some guys were trying to present their bait to the cobia in awkward manners. The insane man in my shoes said, "Stop doing that. You'll spook it!" They reeled in immediately. Again, self-preservation kicked in.

13

I flipped the pinfish slightly ahead of the cobia. The cobia noticed the sound and saw the pinfish. After a second of orientation, the pinfish noticed the cobia. It instinctively fired off the tail after-burners and tried to escape. That movement excited the cobia which swooshed over in a blink and stopped inches from the pinfish. The pinfish likewise stopped. Mexican standoff? Hardly. The pinfish had had a heart attack. Its last reflex twitch jump-started the cobia. The cobia inhaled it. I paused and then set the hook firmly. The cobia felt the sting of the hook and took off like a rocket on the 4th of July to the sound of a singing drag. "Fish On!" I yelled in triumph. "Who wants it?"

A young kid I'd noticed during the day, who couldn't catch a fish if I put it in his pocket, rushed over to me. I put the palm of my hand to his forehead without saying a word, yet saying, "No freaking way," in kid talk. I eyed the guy who unknowingly showed me he had the most experience. When we locked eyes, he came over to me, and I handed Mr. Experience the battle sword. The boy had an opportunity to watch and learn how to land the fish by an experienced angler. Perhaps that lesson was not wanted or acknowledged at the time, yet hopefully, it was taken for the long run.

Yes, the small, under-appreciated pinfish could easily be the start of most of my, and likely your, fishing stories. As in life in general, we don't recognize the value of common things until they're gone. We take things for granted. For example: electricity that lets us sleep well below a ceiling fan, running water so you can read this in your library complete with single flush-seat, a lifelong friend you lean on during tough times, a puppy that angered you by chewing up one well broken-in boot which turns out later to be a sympathetic late-night buddy when you're down in the dumps, or a cat that lays in your lap as you watch TV alone, making you feel like you are not by yourself. You can add to the list.

For now, I celebrate the common pinfish. It has given us many a day of great fishing.

After a day of offshore fishing, if your anchor heading and bearing home are nearly the same by compass, you probably didn't plan your trip well, if at all, and failed to consider the comfort and well-being of your crew.
Salty Dog

The First Time

Dave and his buddies fished with me for several years. They were fun-loving guys. On our first trip, they were somewhat concerned about catching fish. However, the fish catching went well enough that they trusted me with that part from then on. During trips of late, they either reminisced about past school days, ball games, old girlfriends, or caught up with each other's recent times, the good, the bad, and the ugly, as well as their children. Towards the end of the day, they made plans for the next reunion, whether it was taking the families to the beach, going hunting, or our next fishing adventure.

While their fish were cleaned, I'd hangout and recollect the day's fiascos, and a special fish or two. We'd laugh about this and then part company, looking forward to the next trip together.

Dave called in late May to book a trip for him and his son, Zeb, in August when Zeb would be out of school. Zeb was going to be eight years old, and Dave thought it was time to take him fishing. The truth was this; Zeb had seen the photos and videos of past trips and had been bugging his dad to take him. Dave had been telling Zeb he had to get a little older before he could go. Age came naturally, and persistent pestering paid off for young Zeb.

Dave made the call; he wanted to have special fishing time with just his son but didn't want to pay the whole fare. He wanted an eight-hour trip. Gina, my wife, the heartbeat of Big Bend Charters—I just drive the boat—told Dave about the Wednesday Special where various parties can share a full charter. Furthermore, she told Dave she would arrange the other party or parties so Zeb would fit in well. We had a list of folks on standby who loved to fish but liked the individual pricing. Many of those folks would be very Zeb friendly, kind of like an extended family Zeb hadn't met yet. Gina fit everybody together well, and it was a go.

The boat was dressed up and ready when I met Dave and his son at River Haven Marina. I shook hands with Dave, said a few words, and then bent over a bit to address Zeb.

Dave told Zeb, "This is Captain Brian, and he is going to take us fishing today."

I put my hand out. Zeb put his inside my palm while looking down. He was bashful.

"Daddy, I have to use the bathroom," Zeb said. Dave and I walked Zeb around to the men's room. While we waited outside, Dave told me Zeb was so excited about going fishing, it was all he had talked about for two weeks. He also told me he wasn't shy and would get over it once he became familiar.

Dave was right! Within an hour, Zeb had more questions than a game of *Trivial Pursuit* and more charm than Paula Deen at a butter convention. The kid was cool.

Gina had set up the charter very well. The other four people were two older couples that would just as soon catch Florida snapper as anything else. Florida snapper—white grunts—are kid friendly. They are abundant, enthusiastic biters, and delicious fried golden brown.

Looking over the folks fishing with me that day, I knew it was going to be a fun trip. Nobody wanted to deal with a "reef donkey" amberjack or have grouper rock them up. They just wanted to catch fish and have a great time!

Out of habit and never wanting to miss an opportunity, I stopped on the backside of a sandbar over some spotty grass bottom to pick up a quick, dozen pinfish and pigfish for the livewell on the way out. That intentional dozen ended up being two-dozen plus because Zeb couldn't control himself while catching fish. If we had stayed there the entire day, Zeb would have never stopped fishing and never stopped talking about it.

It took a while to promise and sweet-talk Zeb into going elsewhere to catch more and bigger fish. Actually, Dave had to finally tell Zeb to give the mate his fishing pole. He gave it to Casey after one more.

"Zeb, we have a twenty-five minute ride before we start fishing again. You can take a quick nap in one of the beanbags if you want."

That was like asking a hummingbird not to fly. Zeb sat beside me and told me about every fish he had ever caught, including his big catfish…for all twenty-three minutes.

16

The area I headed for was a large piece of live bottom growing on top of flat lime rock. It was a submerged marine, Florida snapper forest, the guaranteed fish grab everybody wanted, but especially Zeb. Casey put out the anchor, set a five-gallon bucket mid-cockpit to toss fish in, and then cut-up a double handful of squid into strips the size of an index finger. All the poles were pre-rigged with simple knocker rigs— an egg sinker of appropriate size, loose above the 1/0 long shank hook. Casey and I baited everybody up. When their bait hit the bottom, it was a three count or less before the bite.

Zeb went to a level of Zen fishing I wish I could attain. Dave didn't have time to fish, though Casey was tending to the others while I was Zeb's personal fish attendant. Dave loved the fishing time with his son. I was in the background, taking care of incidentals such as de-hooking fish, occasional hang-ups, re-rigs, some hook baiting, and shots on Dave's phone-cam. Zeb had Dave and I hopping around him, but he didn't realize it.

It didn't take long for the five-gallon bucket to fill to the point fish could flip out. When that happened, Casey or I tossed the fish into an iced fish cooler. It was hot action fun!

I asked Casey to lay out a pre-rigged kingfish rig off the stern. He did so, using one of three blue runners we caught bait fishing. That pole was forgotten about during the Florida snapper action.

When the action slowed, we re-anchored. We did that twice. Each time, I reeled in the kingfish rod while Casey took care of business on the starboard side, and Dave took care of Zeb.

On the third anchor drop, I had positioned the boat up current of a relatively large, lime-rock structure. Bait fish were hovering above the rock pile. Florida snapper fishing was fast and furious when the lonesome kingfish rod bent double. The clicker alarm clock screamed as line sped off the reel.

It was Dave's time to fish. Casey and I had intentionally placed the king rod in the stern rod holder on Zeb's side of the boat. Dave stepped behind Zeb and grabbed the singing reel. I didn't need to coach him; he knew how to handle the situation. I got Zeb to reel up. The others did so voluntarily.

Dave was off to the kingfish race. Casey got the gaff. I was sticking rods out of the way. Everybody was focused on Dave and the big fish of the day. Zeb was watching and learning as Daddy handled the big fish. His dad performed quite well, giving a fine lesson to his son, although he didn't realize it at the time.

We identified the fish the first time it swam by the boat. It was a kingfish. It was a rather large kingfish. The king swung by twice more and ran off. It was thrilling.

Zeb was a hyper, automatic, word-firing machine around his dad. However, his dad was locked into a world of silent battle. I took Zeb aside to answer the barrage of blather.

The fish tired, and the fight came closer to the boat. The fish burst left, then right, but not as long as at first, just quick roll-offs from a loosened drag. It was Casey's time to shine. The young, eighteen year old had to make the decision about when to stick the fish. He did it in an experienced instant. The gaff tip poked through both eyeballs for the perfect gaff shot.

While others were admiring the fish, I fist bumped Casey, telling him it was a great gaff shot. Zeb was bouncing around his dad. Dave loved the attention from his son. The king weighed thirty-eight pounds. Big enough that everybody got some steaks, even Gina and me.

Zeb was double hooked on fishing. He kept loose math and determined he caught the most fish, and he thought his dad was a superstar, the show-out fisherman on the boat that day.

Take your kids outdoors. It is better than getting them out of jail.
Salty Dog

Blink

The clear blue skies of the early July evening were slowly getting painted—pastels of orange, red, pink, purple, and other colors most guys don't know the names of. The sun silently dipped toward the horizon like some brilliant, celestial tea bag into a vast Gulf of hot water. The suspended particulates held in the atmosphere were mostly invisible when the sun was high, but when the sun was low they became glorified. The skyline bloomed, but the glory was short-lived. One had to make time to admire the event, because it didn't wait. I got a cold drink, sat on the fish-box, waited for, and watched the show. Twenty minutes later, it was over. I walked away feeling rather small. The important events or troubles in my life felt relatively insignificant, considering the big picture. It was time well spent. It was humbling. I came away with a reverence for God.

The morning was spent dodging storm cells—powerful, individual, pop-up systems that developed or, better said, came to life when rubbed together before your eyes. They were awe inspiring, like a sunset, but not something you wanted to sit and watch and be overtaken with. Blazing lightning bolts, each as unique as a snowflake signature, signed an ever changing, moving, dark-to-black backdrop. The recoil of thunder afterwards was a great, fearful voice telling me to run away.

It was a scary game. If we were playing dodge ball, we would have a chance of grabbing the ball and throwing it back, but during dodge bolt, there was just the chance of being hit and taken out of the game—no throw backs. I didn't want to make print in the annual Coast Guard boating accident accounts, so in an effort to avoid making the report, I took us wandering around in the Gulf of Mexico from the safest distance possible till well past noon. I was being a seafaring Noah with an ark of seven individuals looking and waiting for a rainbow promise.

We didn't get much fishing in until after two o'clock. That's when the sky cleared, and the wind stopped completely dead. In the still calm, the Florida broiler turned on above our heads, and the humidity got so thick we were breathing thin, hot water. Sweat rained from the top of my head, rolled down the crease in my back, trickled through the crack of my butt, forked, and ran the length of both legs, collecting little sweat puddles on the way down my calves. It eventually made it into my Croc boat shoes and was squished out the shoe holes with every step I made to form a tiny stream sternward out the scuppers to the open sea. It was a strangling mix of heat and humidity. It was draining. The tick of time and the drip of sweat became a synchronized hourglass, squeezing the juice of life from each of us.

During the storm events, we weren't thinking about drinking water, hydration issues. We—me mostly—were more focused on the situation in front of us, to both sides, and often behind us. But when the sky cleared and the broiler kicked high, I started pounding sixteen-ounce bottles of water. Ice-cold water on a hot boat is better than an ice-cold beer with oysters on the half shell. Well, at least it's better for you; it's hydrating. In the heat, sweat was spouting out of me like each pore was a sprinkler. I couldn't drink fast enough to keep up with the loss.

Sometimes it's just as good to pour water on you rather than in you. I grabbed a towel, dunked it overboard, and rung it out over top of my head and then wiped down any exposed skin downward, including my calves. It felt great! It felt great, when my clothes mopped up the excess, to let me wear the wet rag until it soon dried up. Evaporative cooling is a wonderful thing. Others saw what I did and followed suit, passing the towel around the boat.

We continued working our way to the southwest overtop one good piece of bottom to the next, just parking the boat—no wind or current so no anchor necessary. We left each spot just before it got too uncomfortably hot...ten minutes, fifteen tops. There was no need to let the heat monkey start its mind dizzying dance on anyone's back. We drank water during the intentionally slow rides to the next spot, letting the light mechanical breeze chill us on the go.

Apparently, the fish felt the same heat stress; the bite was nonexistent. It was Mexican Gulf siesta time for those above and below waterline. Grouper fishing was a waste of time in the dead calm heat.

Maybe we were both waiting on the reprieve of night coolness and the light of the near full moon for activation.

The night pardon was five, long hours away. I suggested a change of target species. There was no point in arguing against the suggestion. The forty-minute run to the Air Force microwave tower gave us all a well-needed, prolonged breeze. The sea had turned flat. My thirty-two-foot Twin Vee ran like it was on rails. Holding onto the wheel was optional.

Every now and then a covey of flying fish blasted out of the water on one side or the other, or a lone-horse ballyhoo squirted from the surface at missile speed and angled away from the boat, as if it were some dwarf billfish. Once, a pod of speckled dolphins leapt their way towards the boat. I slowed down, so they could enjoy playing in the wake as well as to draw out our breeze. There is something securing when dolphins escort the boat; they are like a detachment of marine bodyguards.

The air was a sticky, salty, hot vapor mirror such that although the microwave tower was massive and over a hundred feet tall, at nine miles away, the structure faded in and out of view. The tower stayed in focus once the GPS let me know we were ten minutes from being underneath the neck of the high-tech steel dinosaur.

The tower was a kitchen, harboring vast swarms of various bait fish, intimidating-sized barracuda cruising the perimeter, and schools of amberjack segregated by size; the largest of which could test and bust the best tackle or man they brawled. There was a probability of large cobia that if hooked up, would band a crew together to help the one hooked up land the fish of the day. Then there was the possibly of tricking a mangrove snapper, busy grooming the substructure, with a free-lined shrimp and being lucky enough to get it out and away before the line was cut by shot-glass-sized barnacles. Two-hundred to five-hundred-plus-pound Goliath grouper meandered around the tower base. I had the stout tackle on board, two-hundred-pound test mainline and 14/0 hooks if anyone had the nerve to fish for them by dropping a ten-pound *snack* ninety-five feet below. There were also opportunities for gag and red grouper and red snapper on the bottom, but one had to rip them quickly up, less they became fodder to the Goliaths. The point was to get any of that action. It sure beat sweating out the non-grouper bite.

For half the guys, this was the most distant they'd ever been from land. They repeatedly asked how far out we were as if each mile was an achievement. Every time I answered, there was a sense of Disney excitement—a special feeling everyone needs more of in their lives.

"Let's start off with a bang!" I said. A quarter mile off the tower, while the guys were admiring how tall the structure actually was and getting a minute-by-minute realization of how loud the warning horn was, I clipped on two, handmade tube lures to a pair of TLD 15 trolling outfits. After clicking the boat in gear, the mate and I set the lures back about one hundred twenty-five feet. We could just see the tubes wiggling behind the prop wash. Seeing them was an important aspect of the expected entertainment.

"Ya'll watch those yellow tubes, we're about to have some fun," I said.

One hundred and fifty feet from the tower base, the pure blue water glittered with vast swarms of bait.

"Keep your eyes on the tubes," I re-mentioned, noticing most were looking ahead at the bait and tower. One fellow returned to the cockpit just as boil erupted behind the port lure.

"What was that!" he yelled.

The others turned in time to witness a large barracuda blast the starboard bait. The prick of the hook in its mouth ignited the first of many launches. The first flight shot the fish six feet above the surface in a buck-wild, twisting, water-flinging flight that mimicked a rodeo if a cowboy was trying to ride a two-thousand-pound, snot-slinging fish. The fellow grabbed the pole from the rod holder and started his bull ride. Past boredom and inexperience made the short-lived ride comical. The crew of clowns performing in the boat pen couldn't help cutup. From my perspective, it looked like the man was beating himself with a fishing rod. He felt a sense of loss and relief when the 'cuda finally released itself.

"What was that?" he asked out of breath.

"An aluminum tower guard," I smiled.

We all took time to examine the lure. It was cut up fairly badly but was still usable. Surgical tubing is tough stuff. We got things back together and set the lures back out. For almost an hour, we had a ball with the 'cudas, managing to catch, photo, and release three sizable fish before turning our attention toward something else.

We tethered off to the leeward side of the bulkhead, using a long line, looping one end through the starboard bow cleat. Carefully we approached and passed the line around the strut of a ladder that side of the bulkhead then tied the bitter end off to the port bow cleat, using a weathered, figure-eight knot. That system allowed us to simply undo the line from the port cleat, pull the line, and float back away safely in the current.

Luckily, the anchor rode came taunt, setting the boat just inside the tower's shadow. It was a semi-blind chance and welcomed relief. We watched mangrove snapper pruning the huge brace-work of the tower base. The mate chopped up a couple of handfuls of Spanish sardines and tossed them into the struts. The pieces slowly drifted down. Most of the chunks drifted away, but a few drew the attention of the mangos. The fish nosed up to a piece of meat; waited a bit, and then sucked it in. I rigged up two, medium spinning rods with a single, bronzed #1 hook, and a sardine head and free lined it under the structure. It took several attempts before a finicky mango inhaled the bait. The fish was good-sized but not overly large. The light line was necessary to fool the fish into taking the bait but was too light to pull it away from the barnacle-encrusted steel. It didn't take long to figure the futility of trying to catch them, not just hook them.

Schools of amberjack ran just below the cloud of baitfish. The amberjack action was fair, but not as robust as I'd seen in times past. White, buck-tail jigs drew a crowd of AJ's close to the boat yet didn't entice them to take the jig. At times, an excited jack took the free-lined pinfish we had waiting like a Walmart greeter off the stern. Unfortunately, only one fish made the minimum grade to go in the fish box. However, the diversion was all that was necessary in the first place. Catching a rambunctious amberjack is great fun on medium spin tackle.

The action took our minds off the heat that was relinquishing as the afternoon turned to evening.

"Let's go get anchored up for the night," I suggested.

We had burned over three hours, toying around the tower long enough that the sound of the warning horn had become nothing but white noise. There was an old wreck nearby. I figured it would hold enough red and mango snapper and a few grouper to keep us busy until fatigue took over after midnight.

I worked a tight figure-eight pattern around the waypoint until the bottom mark was best recorded on sonar. The mate was ready with the marker jug when I said, "Now." He dropped it overboard. The jug rotated over and over until the lead hit the bottom.

It is amazing to me that we can invest thousands of dollars into electronics, yet success can be so dependent on a brightly colored jug with a measured amount of twine attached to sufficient lead.

The boat came to rest close to the jug, within a half boat length to the stern. The mate made a short cast using a medium-spinning rig with a jig, snagged the twine, and retrieved the jug.

There is a simple satisfaction in anchoring well. Of course in those easy conditions, anchoring wasn't exactly "rocket science."

The first order of business was to send down three blobs of sinking chum in paper-bags, followed by filling and deploying mesh chum-bags from both the port and starboard amidships cleats. That flipped on the "open" sign; we were in business.

Our gear could best be described as light grouper tackle. A sinker sufficient to just hold bottom, yet not make a dent on impact, and a thirty pound test leader to 5/0 short shank bait hook, sturdy enough not to bend on anything more than what we intended to tangle with. The bait was either halved, frozen Spanish sardines or live pinfish. Two medium spinning outfits were "dead-man" rods, from the stern port and starboard rod holders, baited with smaller pinfish with a pinch of shot two foot above the hook.

A few red snapper went in the box, a couple mango snapper made the grade, and we had three break-offs. Soon red and mangrove snappers began to rise in the chum line. The big ones showed a lot of apprehension. The wreck wasn't a 007 secret, and the mangos displayed the learning curve from previous fishing visitors, but I was hoping nightfall would release some inhibitions. We kept the chum going both top and bottom.

The guys were engrossed in fishing. I sat for my silent sunset sermon, ignoring it all. When the major, natural light bulb went all the way out, the mate and I hung battery powered Coleman lanterns from each outrigger and swung them away from the boat. The conditions were that calm. The light from the lamps kept the open sign on after dark, bringing in the customers. From nine through one o'clock, the bite was steady enough to make up for the slackness of the day's grouper bite. Actually, four, fine grouper punctuated the snapper bite, but the exclamation point was a thirty-some-pound kingfish that snatched a small pinfish from the port-stern pole, and after a touch and go battle, it was gaffed aboard. Without a wire leader or stinger hook, the catch was a blend of luck, skill, and teamwork, the proportions of which varied by the moment. Anyway, it looked good in the fish box and made everybody some excellent fresh steaks for the grill.

A couple of guys fished through the night with liquid help. The rest flopped on cushions, beanbags, or wads of extra cloths for the night. Without the sun, the air temperature dropped twenty gracious degrees. A light breeze picked up that was best felt on the bow.

On my beanbag up on the bow, the cool breeze combined with the slight rock of the boat sent me to wholesome rest. I slept on a thin veneer between two vast wonderments. Above me, a never-ending, dry, black canvas with ever-moving, bright stars that changed it constantly. Below me, an immeasurable, mostly misunderstood, living canvas in the flow of water. Each was an awe-inspiring thought.

Thirty minutes before sunrise, I got up with intention. Predawn is a special time when the fish bite can be hot. I got a medium/heavy-spinning combo and tied on a fresh rig out of habit. For bait, I clipped the tail from a smaller, frozen Spanish sardine and hooked it through the eyes. Looking at the two men sprawled out on the stern seats, I figured the fish hadn't seen bait in at least two hours. A quick glance at the GPS told me the boat was near the wreck, within sixty feet. That was important information. A glance at the fish box let me know the boys had put a few fish in the box while I slept. That was good news. My rig hit the bottom, and I tightened up and touched the line with my forefinger. In less than a minute, I felt a touch. I set the hook. The give and take throb let me know the fish was more than likely a red snapper. The hard tug told me the fish was sizable. When the fish was at the surface, I raised the rod high, swinging the fish over the gunnel. It was a snapper off a magazine cover. I got it quietly in the cooler and dropped a line back down. Ditto! Not knowing what was in the cooler, I stopped because my meal ticket was more than full. On the second fish, one of the guys crashed on the stern seat raised his head but laid back into his never world. I quietly put the fish and rod away not wanting to awaken anyone.

The curtain of night was peacefully giving way to the rising sun. The sky was about to bloom. I sat on the same cooler, awaiting the morning glory. Fishing, for most folk, is merely the flailing act of

25

attempting to gather fish, but for others, it is just an excuse to have a moment on the big canvas, the one between the dry and the wet. I waited for His eyes to blink open and start painting. It was again, another time for me to put things into perspective.

'Tis not all of fishing to fish.
Izaak Walton

Party Crashers

Seven ten in the morning, we slid out the mouth of the Steinhatchee River to face a picture perfect April morning. The sun was barely above the tree line. Of the few clouds, some retained a slight hint of pink while the rest were small, loosely wadded, pure white cotton balls. The air still had spring crispness with just a dash of salt from the Gulf. Glassy, one-foot swells rolled in from the southwest, making the boat rise and fall like a child's carousel. Without effort, the boat sliced through the sea, so I pushed the throttles down well past normal cruise speed, jetting healing salt air into the lungs of everyone onboard. We sped to the bait traps six miles offshore. I could feel it; of all the places on earth to be, this, without a doubt, was the best at this moment in time.

Two miles from the bait traps, we all saw several dozen bait pods dimpling the surface. Their little tails made the water look as if a light rain was falling. When the boat passed, ribbons of thousands of small fish flashed away in a synchronized dance. I felt bad approaching them and breaking up their assembly. Gulls and pelicans were seated on the water here and there amongst the bait parties. The birds reminded me of security members strategically placed at a raving, college football game. The birds drifted along with the crowds of bait, merely watching.

At the bait traps, I cut the motors off. When there was a lull in the chitchat, the sea was incredibly quiet except for what sounded like a faint rain hitting a tin roof. The flickers of small fish tails splashing water was in surround sound. Everyone took a moment just to take it in. Life was all around and underneath us. The party was slowly moving north.

The tranquility of the moment was broken when a wave of hundreds of party fish leapt from the sea and splashed down only for another wave of small fish to do the same thing, but up. The gulls and pelicans took flight and hurried over to the sight. Just as the birds arrived, Spanish mackerel began launching themselves through the party into the air to crash back into the sea. The riot lasted a half a minute or so, stopping abruptly. The gulls picked off the chunks of dead fish left behind while the pelicans bombed the disoriented bait that managed to survive the "Spanish" onslaught.

Things went from a peaceful party to a mob riot in the blink of an eye. It was wild to watch once, but the scenario began to repeat itself from one bait party to the next. When the "Spanish" arrived, it was apparent, because the party panicked. The bait fishes stampeded over top of themselves both in the water and in the air. "Spanish" cart wheeled wildly in the mayhem. Gulls and pelicans changed from floating restfully or gracefully flying to acting like disturbed hornets diving into a rugby scrum, adding to the crazy.

I don't know about everybody, but when I see fish going absolutely nuts, I go nuts. I had four, light spinning rods lying across the supports of the T-top, forward of the console. They were pre-rigged for just such an occasion. The rigging is simple. A quarter ounce Key Largo gold or silver tensile jig is haywire twisted to a twelve-inch section of number one, single strand wire. The wire leader is attached to the ten-pound test main line with an Albright knot. The jig is not heavy so the light fishing gear is required to cast it quite a distance into the feeding fish. Besides that, the gear is sporting; it gives fight to the fish. That's where the fun is in the first place.

Little B, the mate, handed out the rods to four lucky anglers as I went through a hurried how to prate. I ended the discourse with, "It really doesn't matter what you do, as long as you get the jig to the fish. If the fish see it, they will eat it!"

And eat it they did! We hopped around in the boat, visiting one panicked party to the next. When an angler got the jig into a raging fish, the drag sang off. Multiple hook-ups transferred the dance from the fish to the folks as they had to do the "over and under hustle" to keep the lines from tangling. The one-to-three pound "Spanish" were personally training some middle-aged men who hadn't seen a gym since high school. Judging by the hoots, hollers, and smiles, I knew these guys didn't realize they were being exercised. We fish trained that way for an hour before we had had enough. Everyone, including Little B and I, got to hustle a few rounds with the "Spanish." We kept some but released most. It was a great way to start an offshore adventure. We picked up a little cut bait, some food, and a lot of fun in that hour.

I realize many people would not have spent an hour cavorting with some misbehaving Spanish mackerel. "Oh, they're just mackerel. I'm not wasting my time with them!" Some say, "I don't like eating them, anyway."

Goodness, have we completely lost touch with our inner child? You know, the little fellow inside us that originally enjoyed fishing for the pure amusement of playing with fish.

It is exciting to watch a "Spanish" snatch a jig then burn off with it. It is a challenge when the tackle is scaled down. I love doing light-tackle Spanish Salsa dance with multiple partners. In moments like this, "Spanish" are overwhelmingly cooperative, so it is also a fun and exciting time to break out that dusty fly rod and give it a whip. Fly-fishing can become a long, drawn-out series of backcasts. In this situation, it's a few quick backcasts and a forecast off to the races. Whatever the case, it is a fun, light-tackle, fish-teaching opportunity.

I'm not saying make a day out of it or slaughter the limit. Just permit yourself and friends an hour or so of fun with light tackle. Think of it as a warm up session before offshore arm wrestling.

The fellow who said he didn't like eating "Spanish" more than likely was served a fillet that had been frozen. Spanish mackerel has to be served fresh, never frozen, for best taste. "Spanish" are an oily fish, so the cooking method needs to allow the fish oil to drip out. That means grilling, smoking, or broiling is far better than frying. If you try eating it fresh and still don't prefer the taste, then enjoy catch and release, and don't worry about the table fare.

Fish with your heart, not your stomach. You'll have more fun, less stress, and never be disappointed. Out of the few days we get to fish in our lifetime, it seems a shame to be so concerned with catching a particular type of fish or X number of pounds of fish that we remove the joy from a precious day on the water.

There is nothing that attracts human nature more powerfully than the sport of tempting the unknown with a fishing line.
Henry Van Dyke

Convicted

The mission was to target sheepshead, also known as "convict fish," because they wear black and white stripes and are notorious bait stealers. We were headed toward an offshore wreck. The day was perfectly "bluebird" in the middle of March. A cold front had passed through a couple of days before, and another was on the way, but this day was cloudless with slick water. Although we were bundled up like skiers on the lift, the non-Floridian garb kept us in Florida temperatures except for part of our faces. Strangely, the cold blowing across our noses felt refreshing, lively. Twenty-five minutes into the ride, I stopped for a nature call and wiped the tears that had been pulled from my eyes. There was a trickle of water from the corner of each eye to the associated ear.

The second leg of the journey went by quickly. During that time, I noticed the water clarity. At twenty-five knots, I was seeing the bottom, thirty feet below! Was this saltwater, or was I running across gin? The cold, winter weather had forced the phytoplankton to fall out of the water column, turning it gin clear. Water that clear makes the bottom machine not necessary; one of the nice things about that is you can compare what is being displayed on the screen directly against reality.

The GPS calculated the wreck site to be two hundred feet ahead on a two hundred sixty degree heading. That was pretty much straight ahead. For some reason, I peeked around the console. Astonished, I could see a large, dark spot ahead on the bottom where the wreck should be. The closer we got, the more pronounced the wreck became. I put the motors in neutral, so we would glide directly over the wreck. Inquisitive as a cat, I excused myself to the rail and looked overboard. I could see the hull and rigging as plain as though looking through thick glass. Following my lead, the others went to the gunnels, immediately carrying on about the swarms of fish milling around the wreck. They were sheepshead.

From the other side, one fellow blurted out, "What the @#$% is that?"

I went over just in time to see the tail section of a huge fish jutting out a hole in the starboard bow before the boat moved forward, and it went out of view.

"That is the resident Jew fish," I said. Goliath grouper for the PC minded, but I said Jew fish because I believe PC stands for Political Coward.

"How big do you think that fish is?" was the rifled question.

"Over three-hundred pounds, American," I responded.

The fish looked like the backend of a Volkswagen partially parked under the cover of a sunken shrimp boat. If seeing something like that ain't cool, then I don't know what cool is.

The sheepshead were as thick on that wreck as sand gnats on a bald man's head during a warm sunset. The wreck had what looked like flowing hair…hair the bald man wanted but wished didn't bite. Folks were excited, waiting to drop bait to the mass of fish, me included. I still get as excited about fishing as when I was a kid on a creek watching carp suck chunks of bread from the surface. It is the feeling of being fully alive; no drug can ever duplicate that feeling.

The fishing poles were pre-rigged. The mate had cut a pile of frozen shrimp into three-quarter-inch pieces if they were large enough to slice. All that was left to do was anchor well. That was up to me. But if it didn't work out well the first try, I'd blame the mate for dropping the anchor in the wrong place. Captains can be so vain. However, no one believes me in the first place when I point a verbal finger at the mate, especially when he gives me another finger back because he has to pull the anchor. It's just for yucks; no harm no foul.

We dogged the anchor rode off due to the lack of sea, and the boat came to rest ten feet, or so, on the port side of the sunken boat. It was a great job; I felt humbly cocky. It was fishing time! Little B, our mate, had everyone baited up quickly. Everybody was more than ready to drop bait on that wad of fish.

The outfits were trout gear, ten-pound mainline, twenty-pound leader, and ended with a quarter-ounce jighead. The lightweight jighead allowed the bait to sink slowly through the fish, giving time for them to notice the bait going down, following it before it became part of the

31

bottom where they would have to hunt it. The technique worked like a charm. The exciting part was being able to watch it work. The angler knew he had a bite before he felt it because he watched the fish eat the piece of shrimp. Sometimes what he thought he saw hadn't happened yet, and he jerked the jighead away. Sheepshead are Houdini fish; they escape more times than not, taking what you had right before your eyes, and getting a freebie from your own back pocket, wrist, or hook. It didn't matter when or how often that happened, because the bite was so steady, a lost fish meant laughter.

The cooler filled up faster than we cared for it to happen. Little B and I were somewhat happy when it was over because our hands were well-used pincushions with little red dots on fingers and palms. The ride back in was a glorious celebration, so much so, we didn't notice the chill. The temperature hadn't raised much during the day.

Seeing the wreck, watching the fish, watching the fish take the bait twenty plus feet below, catching fish on light tackle, a mate doing an outstanding job keeping folks fishing at a fast pace, and the good attitude of some fine folks made the day unforgettable. We were privileged to watch a fish factory at work. The conditions of the day were such that I wish they would happen every time. Every time out isn't that blessed, yet every time out is a blessing.

On the way back in, I started thinking of what we did. I was happy because it was a lot of fun, yet in the back of my mind.... I knew the fish were spawning, producing more fish. I watched some of the large females leak eggs from the vent as they was tossed in the fish box. My thoughts were interrupted by conversation. But back at the dock, my thoughts came back to me as I watched the fish cleaner dress the fish. Large double sacs of eggs were washed down the shoot. Broken egg sacs spewed gobs of eggs all over the cleaning station. They were rinsed away to create clean space for the next fish to be cleaned. I didn't feel happy about that; the future was being rinsed away in front of me. I didn't have to allow killing the egg-laden females to make the day. If they had been released, it would have prolonged the fun. I failed to look at the big picture; that was the way I felt. I thought about the other guide boats that could easily haul in sixty to over ninety reproducing fish per trip per day. I didn't want to be a member of that club. I was convicted.

I delved into the biology of sheepshead to get some footing on my feelings. The common weight is one to eight pounds with an average weight of three to four pounds and a record weight of twenty-two pounds. I can't imagine a goliath twenty-pound sheepshead; the fight would be awesome! A twenty-pound sheepshead might be a fish of the past, but it could be a realistic, future management goal.

Sheepsheads spawn from February through late April here in Steinhatchee, Florida. Females drop, on average, eleven-thousand eggs, if inshore, and two-hundred-fifty-thousand eggs, if offshore, per spawning event. The female may drop this amount of eggs several times per spawning season. Intermittent spawning is an insurance policy that some spawn will occur during the most favorable conditions. All the eggs are not deposited in the same basket. Eggs hatch within twenty-eight hours when the water temperature is seventy-three degrees. Large females may deposit well over one million eggs per season. The males are sexually mature at three years. The females need four years yet grow more rapidly than the males. Their female lifespan is twenty plus years, meaning, left alone, they will reproduce for sixteen years, producing more than twenty million potential offspring. The juveniles mature in estuaries with a diverse diet including crabs, shrimp, and marine vegetation. Perhaps, we should use lettuce for inshore sheepshead bait? Upon maturity comes the call-of-the-wild to spawn. They hear the invitation to join the seasonal, late winter to early spring, migration sheepshead love-in.

In times past, mostly commercial fishermen discovered the secret and took advantage of it for decades. Back then there weren't enough fishermen or enough domestic demand to apply significant spawning pressure. Offshore boats weren't common or desired by recreational fishermen. Now the pressure has become oppressive to the spawn due to the affordability of small offshore vessels and that is in tow with the mobility of fishermen who live inland and trailer their boats.

Furthermore, advances in electronics which can both find and show a beer can on the bottom have allowed the unveiling of most of the past secret sheepshead spawning areas. When spawning sheepshead develop a voracious appetite, they're very easy to catch using shrimp or fiddler crabs as bait. A vast multitude of recreational anglers take advantage of that easy bite and greedily take every fish they can, even to the point of double or triple dipping. That means taking multiple trips out during the same day and harvesting the daily bag limit each time. Greed, one of the seven deadly sins.

I had my conclusions. Fisheries management that allows fishermen to hoard during a determinant spawning period fails to take into consideration the longevity of a specific fishery. Closing sheepshead fishing during their spawn would be initially unpopular, yet the preliminary feelings would fade once anglers started picking up more and more sheepshead in the creeks while red fishing. Perhaps a more agreeable solution would be to reduce the bag limit from fifteen to five and have a brief closure during the peak of the spawn. Regardless, harvesting mature, egg-laden females is senseless whatever the fish species, whether it be sheepshead, trout, redfish, offshore red snapper, or grouper. Why cripple our children's future fishing? After all, a large female sheepshead isn't that much of an admiral prize. Would you hang it on your den wall?

Sheepshead fishing is pure fun. Tossing back the big girls teaches a prudent lesson for those aboard, especially the youngsters. It is a win-win situation.

Governing ourselves is better than being governed. Government management is an oxymoron that has historically proven to be poor, regardless of the issue indulged.

Everything in excess is opposed to nature.
Hippocrates

Funability

The weather forecast was for a very pleasant spring day. The NOAA (National Organization Against Anglers) government approved sea *forecast* released, to us the public, declared a perfect day to come. That authority is known to be wrong so often that if they were running the odds in Vegas, Vegas would have long ago been a ghost town. I always keep that reality in mind. After all, it is my life, as well as those on the boat with me, on the line if the government atmospheric and/or marine speculation is miscalculated. We are the ones who may pay the ultimate price due to another weather misjudgment while they, operating from cubicles inside a no window, hurricane proof building, just push a button to electronically file away one more non-scrutinized prediction.

I'd rather believe conjecture based on the roll of chicken bones from a renowned Voodoo Lady than completely trust the unaccountable interpretation of complex, computer-generated weather data by a mishmash of professional meteorologists. At least the Voodoo Lady would look me in the face and seem sincere.

I mull over the NOAA forecast but factor in decades of experience to come up with my own guess. My forecast is based on true weather representing factors such as reading clouds the day before, my friend Tom's sinus issues, and Internet check points, such as current situations at sea and land weather stations, radar, and reading the lines of barometric isobars. None of my checks have the ability to misinform. When the clouds are high and ruffled, quilt-like to the west, bad weather is coming in twenty-four to forty-eight hours. Bank on it. When my friend's sinuses drain and his eyes puff, there is going to be a significant drop in barometric pressure—translation, foul weather. He is unblessed with a no doubt nose. Weather stations don't transmit opinion, simply information. I like to decode myself. Radar does not lie, and now it is color-coded for ease of interpretation. If isobars are close together, there is going to be an atmospheric fight you don't want to be under.

The weather was going to be picture perfect according to Uncle Sam and, more importantly, to me. We sped across the Gulf toward an offshore bank where I had two bait traps waiting. The traps were set in six feet of water over a patchy sand and grass baitfish haven. The exact location of each trap was marked on my GPS, and by a bleach-white, eight-inch Styrofoam buoy tethered to each trap by a half-inch nylon line.

Protocol was for me to slowly slide amidships close on the windward side of the buoy so the boat could not drift over the trap line, potentially getting entangled in the props. Then the mate, using a long handled gaff, could snag the line under the buoy, pull the line to within hand grasp, and hand line the trap in the boat. Normally, while the mate was hand pulling the trap, it would glitter in wads of living silver just below the surface. At the surface, the little fins splashed making it sound like rain was coming aboard. It is easiest to sort the catch by dumping it all on the deck.

The fish we wanted for bait quickly went in the ready livewell; other fishes went overboard. The crabs crawled about going back last because they could survive the longest out of water. During that time, I identified all the fish and crabs caught for those interested. It was kind of an improvised, marine biology lesson. And then we went fishing.

The six guy charter, me and Jason, the mate, were pumped to go offshore fishing. It was a twenty-minute bait run. I had the glittering bait traps in the back of my mind the whole way. We were all engaged in lighthearted conversation. The kind of conversation that might bust out in full laughter at any given moment…and did. It seemed too quick, but the GPS indicated we were three hundred feet away from the first bait trap, so I slowed down and pointed the bow towards where the eight-inch Styrofoam marker buoy should be. We idled up; we looked around hard for it and determined there was nothing there. We went to the other one, and it was gone as well. We could see to the bottom; the traps weren't there. A boat hadn't accidentally run over my markers and cut the line, leaving the traps below. My bait traps had been stolen.

If someone needed bait, I'd give it to them. If they needed my trap, I'd loan it to them, but I hate a thief. I couldn't and didn't hide the way I felt about that.

So first thing that morning, it was necessary to have six grown men hook and line fish for their own bait. I didn't plan on that. At least five-dozen pinfish were required to make the day, ten live baits per person. I had six, lightweight trout rigs onboard. It took Jason and me fifteen minutes to rig the poles with long-shank bream hooks with a pinch of shot eighteen inches above the hooks and to cut large, dog-claw-sized squid strips to start bait fishing.

I was apologetic to all the men for having to spend their time catching their own bait. Amazingly, they didn't even consider it an inconvenience; they made it into a contest. I didn't identify with how they were having so much fun catching fish no bigger than their own hand, but I wasn't going to rock the boat. The boat was happy. Happy is good.

The pinfish and pigfish bait we needed were at least half hand sized. Big bait was hand sized. The benefit of hook and line bait fishing is catching quality bait you normally wouldn't catch in a trap, for example, catching a few zippy blue runners. They are one of the top ten best baitfish period; you can't even buy them around here. They are the Jack Russells of the baitfish world, so energetic they behave as if dipped from a livewell spiked with speed. They are "money" bait however used, top to bottom. The crew also caught ladyfish and lizardfish that went directly in the bait cooler. They make fine, fresh cut bait, best served in steak cuts. I think of serving a fresh ladyfish steak on a hook as a glittery—scales snowing off on the drop—hors d'oeuvre which could be served at a country bar or star branded restaurant and thoroughly enjoyed by most. On the other hand, lizardfish are an irritating, loathed reef dweller, equivalent to Eddie Haskell from the *Leave it to Beaver* era, with which no other reef fish associates. However, the tang of fresh lizardfish steaks on the bottom sends out a signal to eat for revenge. In other words, fish might eat a chunk of Haskell even if they're not hungry. That is great bait!

Jason and I had been rough counting the bait going in the livewell. "Well, guys I think we've got enough to go fishing," I said, hinting it was time to wander off toward the horizon. I was more than ready to go, still focusing on my stolen bait traps and resenting the need to do this because of some low-grade thieves.

"Captain, can we keep doing this for ten or fifteen minutes longer? John over there has caught not only the biggest but the most, and we can't let him win both categories."

I was thinking how this bait catching detail was erasing time from the day's big hourglass. I was naïve to the counter-current happening, but the soft, underlying vocal and facial nuances I interpreted from a couple guys helped me get up to reality speed. These guys not only were keeping up with quantity but the quality prorated, based on how Jason or I described the value of each baitfish species. They were intent on having fun while fishing regardless of what they were fishing for. The little baitfish were simply one excuse for grown men to laugh and have big fun. They were betting on it, not with money, but just to win the right to gloat.

"OK, I've got ya'll on a timer of fifteen minutes. Gentlemen, start baiting your hooks," I said, sounding like a NASCAR announcer. Somebody had to officiate. I couldn't bring myself to stop the party. Attitude is the prerequisite to fun.

Catching bait ended up as a short-term bit of fun first thing in the morning. It turned out to be a brief morning wake-up and warm-up ritual that broke up the boat ride offshore.

When they asked for fifteen more minutes to catch bait, once again, I came to face the fact that I couldn't force things to be the way I wanted or change the now. It was best to go with whatever page nature flipped open that day, read it, and deal with it. These guys, unknowingly, were helping erode the last of the old me. The me that etched in stone the highest, often unattainable, expectations for each fishing day from the launch. My best thoughts and intentions were always for folk to catch quality fish—whether it were seasonally catching kingfish amongst bait pods, bragging size cobia off structure, or big grouper or snapper off some far away rocks. However, if whatever I mentally wrote on my daily tablet didn't happen, I found myself somewhat bummed, and often, I'd bring others down with me. My passion for the perfect day could rub some fun out of an otherwise great day.

So before the extra fifteen minutes of bait fishing was over, I mentally dropped my stone tablet overboard. I let the stolen bait traps go, accepted the good time catching bait, and acknowledged what a great bunch of guys I had surrounding me. I was happy, real happy. I became happier when I saw vast schools of bait pods dimpling the surface south to north ahead of the boat as we were moving westerly in thirty-two feet or so of water. Some pods were small, like a king-sized bed, while others were as large as a football field. Most importantly,

Spanish mackerel were attacking many of the bait pods. "Spanish" wasn't a guess, because the sound of baitfish rushing from the surface in a unison of terror would snap your head around fast enough to see a few "Spanish" airborne.

I stopped the boat. We wanted a taste of that action! "Jason, get the—" Jason was already grabbing the trout outfits we used to catch bait. While he was cutting off the baitfish rigging, I sat a container of quarter-ounce jig heads and a spool of thirty-pound, test-monofilament, leader material on the captain's bench. Both of us began whipping two-foot leaders on each combo as fast as two, rough-fingered fishermen could orchestrate to the background soundtrack of thousands of feeding fish. The jig bodies were colored glitter silver that best matched the baitfish.

"OK here's the deal. I'm going to run the boat fast towards a school of bait that is being blasted. Right before we get there, I'm going to kill the motors, and we'll coast into the action. Be ready for a sudden slow down, watch your backcast, play well together, and work the jigs quickly in short erratic pops. We're going to bounce from one active pod to the next." That was my spiel to the crew as Jason and I were putting things together, using a dual set of excitedly shaking professional hands. For those that noticed our shaky hands, they confirmed Jason and I were just as enthusiastic about fishing, if not more so, than anyone else.

The boat I run is a thirty-two-foot Twin Vee center console with a twelve foot beam powered by twin 250 hp Suzukis. For my area, Steinhatchee, Florida, it is one awesome fishing machine—not paid or endorsed to write that—for many factors. In this case, the spacious bow platform allowed three healthy men to fish up there, two on either side just behind, and one working the cockpit at will.

The three men on the bow took a knee holding onto the railing. The other three secured themselves until I killed the motors and we skidded in. While still in forward motion, they jumped to their feet and started slinging the jigs into a froth of fish. Some jigs were taken after just getting damp; others were taken at the boat. Some needed to be re-cast, and every now and again, a jig would get clipped off. Jason was busy netting and de-hooking fish. I found myself helping Jason and tying on new jigs for those that got cutoff. We were all in the business of catching fish, and business was good.

Now, using a thin #1 wire leader would have prevented some of the cutoffs, but wire leaders can reduce the action. Action is fun. Why reduce fun? I can tie on a new jig in less than a minute. How many minutes of our lives are spent absorbed in the spirit of fun?

Spanish mackerel give a hotrod fight, taking line in fast bursts. Every one of the guys had numerous shots and successes. The action was so hot they couldn't keep up with whom, how many, or what size, so it was just good, chaotic excitement.

However, on three occasions, something large snatched the jig and took it for a long ride, almost spooling the reel before cutting away. The fish that did that wasn't a "Spanish;" it was, more than likely, its larger cousin the king mackerel. The kingfish are common to run amongst the "Spanish" when food is plentiful; "Spanish" can be king food as well. I filed that action toward game plan next. I noticed there wasn't much floating grass on the surface.

After icing down a couple dozen "Spanish," it was time to change things up. "Spanish" are a fish best served fresh never frozen. The guys didn't want to quit, but when I promised a chance at the big fish they never slowed down. They bought into the deal.

While they gabbed about what had just happened and snacked, Jason and I tied quality, ball-bearing snap swivels onto four Penn 4/0 combos spooled with fifty-pound monofilament. We set the reel drags light enough so the initial strike wouldn't tear the lure away from the fish. I decided to use two Rapala CD 18s and two Rapala CD 22s. All plugs were tiger-striped in black over blue backs with off-white bellies. Those lures were relatively large; unlikely to be hit by Spanish mackerel, they best mimicked the "Spanish" themselves and were designed to dive below the bait schools where the kings would most likely be lurking.

"OK here's the deal. We're going to troll for kingfish, using these four plugs. The two larger plugs, CD 22s, dive deeper and are going to be set back short from the port and starboard stern corner rod holders. The other two plugs, CD 18s, run slightly shallower, and will be set further back and placed in these rod holders forward along the gunnel. This is how we're going to pull this off. Two guys have to sit out. I'll need a man for each rod. Simply mash your left thumb against the spool and flip the lever to take the reel out of gear while keeping the lure out of the water. Those in the stern, point the rod tip out the back; those forward, point the rod tip away from the boat. When I say. "Go," everyone releases the line, keeping slight pressure on the spool to prevent backlash, letting the lure drop into the water. The forward movement of the boat will move the lure away from the boat. When I say, "Stop," the first time, the guys in the back flip the reel in gear and set the rod in the holder, while the two other guys continue to let out line until I say, "Stop," the second time. Then they flip the reel in gear and set the rod in the holder. When a fish is on, the rest have to reel in quickly to prevent tangling. Got it?"

They all said something like, "No problem." It took three tries before there was no problem. I won't go into details, but I needed a chalkboard and colored chalk. Frustrating? No, hilarious.

My inane trolling method from the collective "Go," the first "Stop," and then the second "Stop," was a simple means to make necessary balance. During those commands, I was silently counting down so that the CD 22s and CD 18s were running one hundred ten to one hundred fifty foot astern, relatively.

The weather remained relaxed; small white popcorn clouds dotted a Carolina-blue sky, and the sea was a delicately faceted, undulating mirror. Those conditions kept the baitfish up top, prolonging the mackerel feed. At a five-knot speed, I cruised us around the outer limits of the harassed pods. Within ten minutes, one of the stern poles was yanked down as we trolled by a mass of bait. Kingfish! But the fish didn't sprint. It just kept the rod tip pulled down steady, pulling drag. Didn't anybody else notice?

"Somebody take the rod!" I shouted.

The six guys were politely discussing who should have the opportunity to reel in the fish like they had graduated from the Emily Post School of proper fishing etiquette. I wanted six year olds grabbing for the last candy bar. I put one arm around the guy closest to me and speed walked him toward the pole. Jason had already pulled the pole from the holder, turned the drag a bit tighter, and handed him the pole. "Go!"

"Ya'll got to reel in the rest of those lures, now!" Everybody snapped back to reality.

The fish was a brawler, fighting in short hard digs. Jason said, "Grouper."

I nodded in agreement. A fine, twenty-six-inch gag grouper came to the gaff. After a short celebration and some photos, one guy said smiling, "Captain, you said kingfish."

"Yea, what do I know? It's my first day on the job." Even Jason

41

laughed at that response. We ended up catching two more nice grouper, trolling.

We were trolling a fair distance between two large bait pods, basically, just killing time going from one to the next. I ball parked troll time to be fifteen minutes before we'd be close to the bait and then, maybe, action. Everyone knew we were in the middle of nowhere, so we were shooting the breeze not paying attention to the trolling rods.

"The watched pot never boils." The forward port rod dragging the CD 18 snatched down, and the sound of line boiling off the reel was violent and didn't let up. That alarm started a firemen's scramble in the cockpit. Thankfully, the crew had got over that "Emily Post" nonsense and was turning into a semi-pro pit crew.

"Clear the rest! Clear the rest!" Jason was shouting to hasten the guys in pulling the other gear out of the water and out of the way. Once collected, Jason stowed them neatly on the rod holders forward on the T-top.

"Wally, let it burn baby; let it burn," I was saying to the man with fish on, encouraging him not to buck the fish but to let it *Rage* the reel drag. "Keep the rod at the eleven o'clock position. Let it fight the rod and drag," I said, instructing him to raise the rod.

Two minutes later, "The fish is off," said Wally with slack line swaying toward the water.

"No it's not! It's running at the boat. Reel fast! Wally, reel faster, like you want the fish! Never give up until you see your hook with no fish on it."

His friends cheered him to step on the gas and turn the reel handle quickly. Thankfully.

I'd trolled for kingfish for many years, more than my, "First day on the job," and through experience could read the response of both rod and reel. I knew the drag tension and approximate distance the fish ran off with the lure. The fish that had the lure in its mouth was probably a kingfish, a large kingfish, a "smoker," for my Steinhatchee area.

I returned to the helm, bumped the boat forward to help suck up some slack that Wally couldn't pick up on the wind. The forty-foot bump forward helped get Wally's line tight. The taut line zipped by the starboard side, riding up a thin string of water blowing behind it. Nobody saw the fish; it was running deep, fast, and passing the boat.

You don't want to fight an express fish from the bow. If it reverses, you may not be able to back up fast enough. I wanted the fish off the side or, better yet, off the stern quarter; that way I could best use the boat as a tool. I kicked the boat slow, hard port by putting the starboard motor just above idle speed, while placing the port motor in reverse, tethering the reverse speed. That maneuver rotated the boat from right to left, changing the fight position sternward. Then I put the motors in neutral and waited for what the fish was going to do next. The fish ripped a half inch of line off the spool at a blinding pace and headed straight back.

Jason slipped his hand in from behind Wally, tweaking back his reel drag, loosening it to adjust for the added pressure of the line being hauled through the water. Just the resistance of the line moving through the water could generate enough force to tear the hook away from the fish. Jason's quick move likely kept Wally tied to the fish.

A good mate is more than worth the tip money. Much of what a mate does is taken care of before arrival or after folks depart. Some is taken for granted; a little is seen and appreciated, too little in the deserved limelight. Jason was so smooth, I had to make a point *to point* out the *little* things, often unnoticed, he did to make the big happy happen. I wanted him to make good money, real good money. After all, he was doing a great job of making us look good, not only during the day, but importantly at the end of the day when the fish were hung up on the board and the photos were taken.

The fight went for another fifteen minutes of give and take. Wally's taking part, getting more than the giving. The whole time I kept the scene sternward. It had been an exceptional fight. Wally had worked the fish near the boat. The fish swam by the port stern close enough for all to see. It was a kingfish! Forty plus pounds of luminous silver with a CD 18 latched to the right side of its head. It was leaning to its left as it swam by with a large pronounced eye. Wally thought it was about over. I reached over and set the drag back a little more.

"It ain't over yet," I said quietly to Wally.

He looked at me oddly. It had been a long fight. The fish was here, and Jason had the gaff in hand. The fish bolted, snatching the rod and Wally's head the same direction.

"They hate boats, and with everybody looking at it, ya'll put way too much ugly in the water and scared it off." I smiled saying that, but it drew some colorful commentary.

The fish bolted off three more times. Each time wasn't as far or as energetic as the last. I turned the motors off and tilted them all the way up to take the noise, as well as the obstructions, out of the equation. The fight boiled down to a slow-speed, pendulum swing on the windward side. You want the boat drifting away from the fish not overtop it. Pressure was mounting. Jason was birddog focused, darting left and right of Wally to get that shot. A gaff is not a tool to dig a fish from below the surface. Use it when the fish is at the surface so as to snatch it quickly out of its element into yours.

"Give Jason room to work," I said in a firm captain's voice.

I've been where Jason was, and the last thing needed was to worry about jabbing somebody with the gaff in the heat of the moment. Besides, the mouth of a king is nothing but an up and down set of razors that will be snapping wildly once boated. Fishing is a blood sport; I like all the blood to be from fish.

Jason felt the moment, took the shot and had the king coming over the gunnel. However, Jason is shorter than average, and the fish was longer than average. He ran out of vertical inches in an instant. He started horizontal movement with the fish tossing on the gaff. I moved around the helm like a linebacker. Jason looked at me, his eyes big. My right hand grabbed the gaff below his, and we pulled the king aboard together. I broke away back to the helm. He maintained control of the fish on the gaff.

Wally stood staring in silence at his prize on the deck, though a party was erupting around him. I noticed Jason had gaffed the fish under the jaw and through the right eye. A fantastic gaff shot, control with no loss of meat. Jason and I caught eyes. I nodded, recognizing the gaff shot. He smiled. Much of the vocabulary of men is silent.

The king was completely worn out. Jason used a pair of needle nose pliers to easily de-hook the fish from the fore and aft treble hooks. It was beautiful. Bucket list for our area.

Back slaps and bear hugs shocked Wally back with the rest of us. There was a cockpit party with guys digging out cell phones. Candid photos were being clicked off at an IP rate. Once things settled down a bit, Wally was the man in the middle holding his prize with a background of that guy or another, a collection beside him. After that was over, Jason and I went on either side of Wally for a web photo. By that time, Wally was struggling to hold the fish up for the photos. So Jason held the head, I the tail, and Wally stood between us with a happy smile, partly relief.

Somebody raised the lid on the fish box, and Jason eased the fish on ice. I looked at Jason; he said "forty five."

I said, "Forty." I'm conservative. Best to make folks happier at the dock than let them down when the true fish weight is announced. At any weight, that was an exceptional kingfish for the Steinhatchee area. Wally was pleased, as were the rest, including Jason and me.

That one fish could easily feed everybody and their families. Kingfish, like "Spanish," are a fish that should only be served fresh. Freezing any mackerel would turn a great eating fish into cat food. The best cooking method is any means that removes the natural fish oil from the fish such as grilling or broiling. Never eat the dark meat; it is very fishy tasting.

We were already set up, so we trolled around for another thirty minutes. Actually, that spin was to give Jason time to prepare the large spinning rods for our next adventure. The prep was simple. He just had to tie on a three-foot section of sixty-pound fluorocarbon leader to forty-pound braid mainline, using "no-name knot" and twist a 7/0 circle hook on the end. Two of the rods were already set to go. The others didn't take long to rig up.

During that time, a CD 22 got hit. Mark was the next in line. Unlike Wally's ordeal, this fish was brought to the boat quickly. Jason snatched the fish aboard by grabbing the lip of the plug, no gaff, and no kill. It was a twelve-pound snake king. After some photos, Mark tossed the fish back to begin our next adventure, amberjack, nicknamed "reef donkeys" for good reason.

We went to "the spot with a hole in it." There was a freshwater spring less than five miles from where we were that was a frat house for rambunctious amberjacks. The livewell full of bait, especially blue runners, was the equivalent of rolling up with a keg and young women.

Jason prepared to toss the anchor; we looked at each other. The conditions, weather, sea, bait, and otherwise were such that effort was unnecessary. Jason and I got together in quiet.

"There is no need to make this crazier than it has to be. Start with two rods, one with a runner and the other with something else. Let's do this off port," I shared to his ear. He took the big net from the bungee that kept it secured to the starboard side of the console and availed it neatly to the stern. A couple of guys caught his maneuver and made comment to the others.

"It's fix'n to happen."

I pushed the boat fifty yards up current, brushed the boat to

45

starboard, shut the motors down, and cut them hard starboard, fixing the drift to fish off port. Jason fished out a blue runner; they were quick, so it took a few scoops from the tank to capture one. He pitched it straight back, placing the rod in the port stern holder. He went to bait the next hook. He almost made it before a boil erupted near where he had tossed the runner. Jason swiftly pinned on a pinfish and tossed it forward, placing the rod in a holder ahead of amidships.

The boil caught everyone's attention. The swash of water we witnessed was way more than that little runner could ever make. That bait was running counter-clockwise, avoiding the life cycle it was flung into. Open field running sent it on a spirited topwater sprint just ahead of the hoard of fans, like it was Elvis scurrying through an airport at the beginning of his heyday. Steve reached for the rod.

"Don't, let it happen; the circle hook will do it," I said, touching his shoulder. The top skipping runner ran out of gas, fell below the surface, the rod yanked down hard, and the drag squealed off. Steve looked at me. "It happened; get it"!

At the same time the other rod got nailed down. Tom seized that opportunity. While moving to the helm I said, "You got to keep them separated." I raised the motors to rid the obstructions. The fish danced, and the men were forced to dance along in reverse like Ginger Rodgers with the moves of Fred Astaire, keeping the lines separated, choreographed in action by Jason.

We boated both fish. They were ballpark same size, "cookie cutter," twenty to twenty-five pound fish. Fish often school by size. These were good fish, great fighters, but far from oversized. Nonetheless, they were everything called for. We needed four more to make the limit, one amberjack per person.

Law doesn't allow captain and mate to include their fish in the limit on charter boats. We are either gifted excess fillets or scrounge leftover heads or remains from the fish cleaning to eat fresh fish. Something like, the government forcing a dairy farmer to buy milk from a grocery store.

Just for the excitement of it, we selected the runners to pole-dance. Men filed in rotations of two to get their private donkey dance. A couple of fish were lost, so it took three rotations before the limit was met. Then we caught and released AJs for a half hour or so of sport fishing. The guys ran out of energy before live bait. The never-ending romp of donkeys spent the men. At the end, they resolved to flip unhooked live baits off the boat just to watch the show beneath, behaving as royals feasting above on meaty sandwiches, chips, and chocolate covered snacks on a floating coliseum as the lions performed below.

As a sideshow, on the way home, I dropped anchor on a large piece of lime rock bottom for yo-yo Florida snapper—white grunt fishing. I don't call it fishing; it's catching. Those grunts are so abundant, they'll turn a first-timer into a self-proclaimed pro in a matter of minutes. That is why I named it yo-yo fishing; the bait goes down on a string, the string bottoms out, the bait spins at the bottom a few seconds. Snap it back up with a grunt attached; repeat until tired of playing.

We did that, using the lightweight spinning combos. The lighter tackle upped the fun factor. Jason assembled each combo with a "knocker rig." With the exception of tying a single hook to the end of the line, the knocker rig was as uncomplicated as it gets. Before tying the hook on, you slip the line through an egg sinker just heavy enough to hold bottom for current conditions, and then tie on the hook and bait it.

> Captains tip: Use long shank hooks for ease of de-hooking. The hook size should be 1/0 or 2/0. The bait could be anything, even mini-marshmallows, but durable is best, such as squid or cut bait.

While en route, Jason dipped out a dozen baits from the livewell that didn't survive, chunked them up on the cutting board, and put the pieces in a plastic container with a handful of ice. Once anchored, Jason added a layer of ice on top of the fish already in the fish box and propped the lid open. It was yo-yo time.

All the guys were fishing in a matter of minutes. Jason and I were quickly overwhelmed, shucking Florida snapper off the hooks, tossing them in the open fish box, occasionally re-baiting. The guys figured out that although Jason and I were working as fast we could, we couldn't keep up with all six. Thankfully, they started DIY tossing their fish in the box.

The fish box was filling quickly at two pounds per toss. A half hour into it, Jason applied another layer of ice. The four-hundred-quart fish box was two inches from full. "How much ya'll want? Are ya'll going to clean your fish or have them cleaned?" I told them the price of fish cleaning by the pound before they answered.

"How much do you think we got?" they asked back. "Between two hundred twenty five to two fifty," I responded in an experienced guess.

"We're going to have them cleaned…we best stop. Thanks for the heads up captain," Wally said for the rest after a brief get-together. "We're done."

The ride in was roughly an hour. There were two, large beanbag chairs on the deck behind and below the bow platform I named Mary Ann and Ginger. Mary Ann was on port, my steering side, because she was my favorite. Anyway, two guys were crashed in each beanbag; one laid himself to rest on the bow, and the last fell asleep riding next to me on the captain's bench. After Jason did a light boat scrub and rinse, he took a deserved power nap on the stern seat.

During the ride in, I kept an eye on the GPS and compass while trying not to run over sea turtles or crab trap buoys and nodding off myself. At the river "NO WAKE" sign, I eased the motors back to slow speed. The sound change woke folks up. For a couple guys, they woke up back in Steinhatchee like Dorothy did in Kansas from the *Wizard of Oz*. "We're back home." The beanbags were horizontal time accelerators.

The day finished on a happy note at the dock. Fish were hung on the board for a quick last photo. "Smile, say cheese," said Gina, my wife, momentarily stalling the yick-yack for clicks from everybody's phone or camera. Then they told of the day to Gina. She eats that up.

Although the first part of the morning didn't turn out the way I expected, I chose not to carry it with me. It was the best choice. The other option offered an excuse not to fish for all we were worth. The point is, with the right attitude, you can fish as hard as you wish, yet relax, have fun with those you are with, and enjoy the day regardless of the outcome; catching the target fish, a bunch of fish, some fish or, God forbid, no fish at all.

I have fished through fishless days that I remember happily and without regret.
Roderick Haig-Brown

Gracie

Gracie was a long blonde-haired, ten-year-old girl, tall and thin, not scrawny or gawky, but surprisingly elegant for her age. The first time her dad, Clint, introduced her to me, she was shy for the moment and clung to her mama, Aunde. Clint had fished with me before as part of group of men. This was the first time he brought his family. After the brief introduction, mom and daughter wandered up to the front of the boat to begin nesting, I whispered to Clint, "In all honesty, in six years, you're going to have to beat the boys away."

He looked back, "I know."

Aunde's overshadowing genetic input insured Gracie wasn't going to turn out a wallflower. Clint seemed to be happy his stuff was lost in the mix.

***

My wife, Gina, and I have no children. We love children. She loves them in numbers to fill a large Sunday school class. I was an only child. I lack experience and confidence to feel comfortable with more than one or two children at a time. Also, I'm most relaxed around boys because I was a boy myself, and while growing up, most of my friends were boys. I definitely relate best with boys.

Little girls befuddle me. For that matter, women do too, but that's a pointless novel. I'm a teddy bear, but a large guy who may initially intimidate young girls. It is a first, high hurdle to friendly jump across. Also, I don't know how far emotionally or physically to push girls, and I have a vague understanding of their skill-sets. If they cry, I feel like the biggest jackass. I'd rather take a punch than have a little girl cry. Then oddly, if I try to hug them to end the tears, they could perceive me as a huge monster that sprang from underneath their bed at night, trying to grab them. It can go from bad to worse in a hurry; much of it is in my head. To compensate, I allow for a slow, warm-up period mixed with silliness and corny jokes. It is obvious when I become OK to them. Then we can play fishing together.

So I was looking at Gracie, contemplating my inhibitions and lack of knack with young girls. I asked Clint what they wanted or expected on the trip, and his response was, "Keep it active."

"She's kind of lean; is she fragile, Clint?" My question was awkward and sounded as such. Thankfully, Clint knew me and could read me between the awkward. He laughed. His laughter was a relief. I thought he might become upset.

"That little girl is as tough as nails, and she will never give up," he stated, and then went on to tell me about her competitive barrel racing on horseback. Clint is not one to embellish. By the time he finished, her fearless horseback riding impressed me. I'm not scared of horses, but I won't get on one. They don't have brakes, and there is no key to turn the ride off. Enough discussed, I wanted Gracie to ride a fish as memorable as any horse she had ever ridden and make a memory that would last a long time.

We started the day, trolling some spoons for Spanish mackerel on the southern edge of the Little Bank, seven miles due west of Steinhatchee Marker #1. Strong winds had stirred up the bottom, making the water clarity less than pure. The "Spanish" bite was "non-active."

A quick, six-minute boat ride put us on a sheepshead spot. Would Gracie be able to detect the subtle peck of a sheepshead bite? Would she be able to catch the fish on the light tackle necessary to feel the bite? Would I have to drop a line and give a how to sheepshead lesson? Answer to question #1: Yes, cat-like. Answer to question #2: No, the light tackle suited her quite well. Answer to question #3: No, better to preach to the choir!

I stood by her, dropped a few hints, and she became quite the professional after two missed pecks. She understood the function of the reel drag, pulled up, and reeled down. She impressed me. I can't recall the number of grown men I've tried to teach that touch, but they barely got the feel after using up four times the normal amount of cut shrimp for a less than average catch.

I told Clint, "She's a natural."

Clint soon jumped in the fun with his daughter. They joked happily back and forth. Double fish were common. Clint would convince Gracie her fish was bigger, stronger, or something extra special. Aunde was a cheerleader mom making sure Gracie was just as caught up as the fish. Aunde thoroughly loved watching Clint and Gracie having fun, but she wasn't a woman who, let's say needed nor wanted to get "fishy" to better enjoy it. She was a hundred pounds of lovely, southern charm.

I sweet-talked Aunde into participating. That took some extra sugar-smack, and the promise she wouldn't have to touch much except clean towels. Even Clint was impressed when she agreed to fish. He volunteered out of fishing to help me, thankfully. Clint hung with Gracie, and I managed Aunde. Gracie was a sheepshead catching machine. Clint was busy de-hooking, re-baiting, and finger bleeding. Aunde was re-looping why she shouldn't be involved with this. I was re-looping a smile and re-baiting. Aunde caught the majority of fish we eventually used as live bait, plus one shamelessly small male sheepshead we released, and one keeper that we all celebrated touchdown style. A fine fish boat limit went in the fish box, mostly stocked by Gracie. I never picked up a pole.

After being an eyewitness to Gracie's skill-set, I was comfortable going to the next level of fish adventure. The boat ride was forty minutes. During that time, mother and daughter nested in one of the large beanbags and picnicked. Clint rode shotgun, and we had a good talk punctuated with laughs.

The livewell was fairly well stocked with a mixture of bait, incidentally caught while sheepshead fishing. They were about to be dropped off in a bad neighborhood. The water was deep and dark, but sonar revealed the anchor came tight atop a stack of amberjack, also known as "reef donkeys." They were large fish for a ten-year-old girl. Actually, they were large fish period. A couple of those rambunctious, gut-kicking donkeys, and I have had my fill. Gracie was in for a challenge. I had forewarned Clint about the upcoming event. It was kind of an opportunity for him to call it off.

"She'll love it!"

I took a medium/heavy, 4/0 grouper combo hooked on one of the largest live baits and free-lined—no sinker—out the back. I placed the rod in the stern port rod holder. The drag set was firm not stiff.

Gracie noticed the bait; it was a fish she'd normally love to catch. Her face showed some bewilderment. Aunde noticed the bait. Her face showed anxiety. She walked up from behind, put her hand on her little girl's shoulder and kissed Gracie on top of the head. Then Aunde gave me the "look." I mentally translated her facial expression as such, "If you, yes I'm looking at you, Mister Boat-driver-man, cause or let anything harm this little girl, my precious baby girl, you're going to think the movie *Full Metal Jacket* was a gay musical."

I was seriously considering reeling in the bait and leaving. Maybe this was too much?

Too late!

The pole jerked back flat. The fish had the pole pinned in the rod holder.

Clint had to twist it to work it free. It took him a few minutes to gather control of himself and the rod. "Come on Gracie!" The next time he called, he looked back to Gracie, "Gracie, come get it!"

Aunde released her grip on Gracie's arm, and she ran to her dad. I couldn't look at Aunde. Mama held her back with strength, but it took more to let go.

Gracie stood in front of her father. Clint wrapped himself around her, holding the pole so that Gracie could get one hand above the reel on the pole and the other on the handle. It was an uncomfortable stance for Clint. When the fish surged, the rod bent down hard, and they stutter-stepped together in an awkward, father-daughter dance.

I raised the motors so the lines would clear props before getting beside the couple in fish action. I do that to coach and/or drop some helpful hints. I was there for Gracie. I didn't care if the fish got away as long as Gracie returned to Mama the same way she left. I recalled *Full Metal Jacket* as a gory flick about the Vietnam War. I walked out of the theater thankful I'd been born a decade too late for call-of-duty to that nightmare. Aunde's look created the atmosphere I was operating in.

Clint hunched over, his chin was just above Gracie's head, and he was continuously speaking in the encouraging language of love. Though some of his suggestions weren't the best advice, I wasn't about to correct anything. I was content to drive a boat so Clint would have an opportunity to wrap his arms around the little girl he loved. It was all under control. I stepped from the sideline. Aunde came in close to cheerlead. She had become more comfortable and joined the game.

On the sideline of the helm, I watched a little girl totally connected with a fish, too large to handle by herself, become entangled in a web of love. At the moment, she didn't realize she was so luckily entrapped.

It was beautiful to be there to watch that develop. Fishing means something different for each person on the same boat at the same time.

Gracie's fish was an average, twenty-pound amberjack, nothing exceptional to show at the dock. Nobody gave a thought about dock début. But Gracie's fish was extra special, because it was a family moment. A moment well celebrated. Everybody got a hug, including the fish. Gracie wasn't shy.

"Can we do it again?"

"You bet," I said while tossing out another hapless bait. The same thing happened. And again plus more. After putting the third amberjack in the fish-box, I said we were limited-out. "Gracie, we can't keep any more fish."

"That's OK; can we keep doing it for fun?"

"You think your dad could try one all by himself?" She smiled OK. Clint caught one. Gracie was happy for him, but she couldn't wait to get back in the game.

She scored twice before I said, "What about your mama?" Aunde immediately said, "No!" And straight away she went into a very polite discourse about how she was so happy the way things were, and she didn't need to catch a fish.

"Come on, Mama. It's fun!"

"I know baby but—" Clint started charming her.

"I know but—"

"Clint will help you just like he did Gracie. If you decide you don't like it, you can quit at any time." Collectively, we coaxed her to give it a reel.

I pitched out a live bait. In minutes, the pole bent over. "Get it Mama! Get it!" Gracie shouted. Clint had the pole in hand.

Aunde started bowing out until Gracie took her by the hand. Aunde took the Gracie stance in front of Clint. He began sweet-talking her through the ups and downs, lefts and rights, when to reel, and when to let it ride. Gracie was chirping in. She couldn't help herself. Unlike Gracie, an exuberant participant, Aunde wasn't so caught up. We could tell by the nice way she kept saying, "I can't do this."

On several occasions, if Clint didn't have both arms tight around her, she would have slipped out, but Clint's snugness and everybody's words of encouragement kept her going. When I said, "Ya'll need to get a room," she cracked up. I knew Gracie was too young to understand. Eventually, we netted the fish. Aunde was happy, but I believe she was more relieved.

"You did it Mama!" was Aunde's real reward.

Gracie took another turn at the reel. And one last time, that turn just as energetic and joyful as the first. She didn't quit because she was tired. The weather was becoming questionable. We started heading in. Gracie plopped in the portside, helm side beanbag chair with her mom for the ride home. They shared a quick snack huddled together and then napped.

The sea kicked up, a light rain started, and the view forward indicated it was going to get worse before reaching the safety of the Steinhatchee River. I stopped the boat. Underneath the center console, I stored odd-sized rain gear, plaid quilted jackets in my size, and a plastic tarp. Clint and I hurriedly worked together to form a warm, plastic encapsulated cocoon for the beanbag duet.

We made do with rain jackets and got butt wet cold from the waist down. The less than forty minute sprint home turned out to be an hour and a half blend of fresh, pelting rain and saltwater spray wallow in the Gulf of Mexico. During that mix, I told Clint he was right; Gracie was tough as nails and never gave up.

By the time we made it back to the dock, the weather had eased off to a dreary, misty drizzle. Aunde and Gracie broke through the cocoon, ruffled as baby chicks breaking from a single egg. Clint and I still looked like the foul weather we had traveled through.

Clint thanked me with a handshake and a man hug. Gracie latch hugged me. Aunde politely hugged me and pecked me on the cheek. That sang volumes, a light lip chorus from a *Full Metal Jacket* musical I never wanted to experience.

Gracie was inspirational. Barring the bad weather on the return, I hoped she enjoyed riding a different kind of horse that day, a "reef donkey."

Nine years later, I came in from a charter and was off loading the boat. I heard, "Captain B." I turned to see a beautiful, tanned, blonde, young woman in a white bikini. "Do you remember me?" She removed her stylish sunglasses.

"You're Gracie, and you're unforgettable!" We hugged.

They are able who think they are able.
Virgil

54

A Few Things I've Found Important

If you do anything long enough, whether you like doing it or not, you'll learn how to do it better and faster by figuring out what is really important and, just as important, what is really not. For example, an experienced heavy equipment operator at a quarry can load more rock in an hour than three new operators can load in a day. His machine is merely an extension of his hand. A good businessman can sort through the clutter, find the bottom line, and call-the-ball during lunch, while someone fresh out of college may need a day or two to take care of the same matter.

I've been fishing for a while—all my life. I've goofed my fair share. Sometimes the knot that I was trying to tie turned into a monofilament wad. I've made backlashes in reels the size of 1970s Soul Train Afros, boat-buying blunders, and more, all the way back to not putting the plug in the boat. If you've screwed up something in regards to fishing, chances are I've done the same thing in triplicate. I remember wrapping a rubber worm around a hook, tossing it out under a cork, and watching for hours before declaring the fish weren't biting. I tend to be a slow learner. Nonetheless, I learned through a long period of unfortunate events. I've gotten "gooder through the badder." I'll review a few things I've learned. I hope these topics save you time and money.

Bait is important! Have you ever gone fishing and forgotten the bait? I have too, but that is not what I'm getting at. Although buying frozen or live bait can save time, it proves to be a poor substitute for fresh caught bait, when available. A fresh caught Bonita for use as cut bait and/or a livewell full of hand-caught cigar minnows, scaled sardines, blue-runners, pigfish, pinfish etc. will, day in and day out, catch more and better fish than any store bought bait. Nonetheless, every time providing fresh bait requires a prolonged period to produce,

I feel pressure. Am I spending time wisely? I've spent an hour and a half catching quality live baits, knowing all the while that bait fishing was chewing into charter fishing time. However, quality bait has proven its worth again and again. Quality bait is worthy of the effort, period.

Think of it this way, if you weren't really hungry and someone put a peanut butter and jelly sandwich in front of you, you'd probably pass. But in the same situation, if you were served a hot apple pie with a scoop of melting ice cream on top, you'd have to take a bite. Fish are the same way. All you want them to do is take a bite. It is always best to serve the fresh pie. However, always bring some frozen-backup bait because sometimes a fried peanut butter and banana sandwich is preferred over a tender steak; maybe it's a universal Elvis thing.

I was flipping through a *Bass Pro* magazine last week. Although I'm the kind of guy who likes to wash and lube his own reels, I was looking at the new featured reels. Actually, I was looking at the standard replacement cost for my old stuff. Anyway, on the pages of reels, I saw some starting at two hundred fifty dollars or more, some between three and four hundred dollars for spin and/or conventional reels, and the new-fangled models were listed at over five hundred dollars! All of these would be commonly used for light freshwater to average, offshore saltwater fishing. None of it was necessarily bragging gear for marlin fishing in some exotic location. I've never been a rich man, so I gasped. Who buys this stuff? We're buying fishing tackle not purchasing precious metal, for goodness sake. Then I read the small print, metals such as gold, platinum, and some materials developed for space travel were used to make some of these reels. I stood corrected.

Crap, I was thinking of a simple mechanism to efficiently roll monofilament line onto a spool, without making a mess and doing it repetitively while lasting a few years in a saltwater environment. There was no need for NASA grade Star Ship Enterprise equipment that required dilithium as a standard necessary developmental material. "Captain Kirk, I can't afford the dilithium reels on my charter boat! We've gone too far."

Honestly, I'd be afraid to hold that much value in my hand just to reel in a fish. If somebody gave me that reel, I'd put it in a safety deposit box and list it in my will. However, some poor guy is going to be sold on it and say to his wife, "Hey Honey, I know the power was cutoff two days ago, but look at this new wiz-bang reel I bought. You can see it sparkle in the candlelight when I place it on the TV tray. By the way, I got one for you too."

A thought: more fish have been landed on a Zebco "pencil sharpener" reel than all the other reels combined. However, if you're an avid saltwater angler, Zebco isn't your reel deal. Buying quality gear is sound, but there is a point of overkill. My gear averages two hundred fifty dollars per combo. I'm not saying it is the best, but it does a fine job and stands the test of John Q Public, day in and day out. My point is this. Before sinking a big chunk of change into one expensive outfit, consider purchasing two, quality, less costly combos. The other could be for a back-up for you or for sharing with friends.

We have all invited a friend fishing who showed up with a well dusted, un-oiled combo with brittle line. It was stored in the cobwebbed rafters of the rusty shed. He bought the combo cheap at a garage sale somewhere. He can't remember when or where. It's better to hand him one of your suitable outfits rather than go through the arduous detail of trying to overhaul what time has eroded or listen to him groan about his crappy equipment during the precious little time you have fishing together.

Did he save money buying something at a discount that wouldn't work when he wanted it to because he never took care of it before needed? He bought something for you to suffer with by inviting him fishing. Again, best to buy a double quality than a single flashy. It is not just for the *him* in your life; it is more for you.

One winter evening, I broke down, in boredom, and read through a book of fishermen's knots. It was time well spent. Although I knew how to tie several good knots, I have found myself thinking, "I hope this knot holds." That is not a comforting feeling. Especially so when you realize how much it cost to get where you are and that you're casting out a line of hope based on a knot you're not sure of. I've seen many people put together some monofilament oddities, but it is far better to learn how to tie the right knot. The knots I use the most are: improved clench, uni-knot, king sling, Albright, No Name, Rapala loop, and the dropper loop. I'm not going to explain how to tie them. You can go on-line to learn or buy a book like I did. I can say, time spent learning good knots is time well spent.

Space…the ultimate frontier…I'm not writing about outer space, but boat space. I, myself, have bought a boat, installed a bunch of equipment, and brought on necessities, then added aboard additional loads of necessities for the day's fishing. By doing so, I have painted others and myself into a very expensive corner of fiberglass. We couldn't move around without stepping over this or that necessity. Sometimes I wouldn't move around the boat to go do that or get something, because it was just too much hassle, or even a safety hazard to step over the safety equipment.

I had to drop back and punt. What do I actually need on the boat? Safety equipment is a must, but can it be arranged better, more simplified and easy to get to? How much other stuff is really needed? I didn't buy any, but somehow, I collected seventeen pints of sun block in twelve different flavors. One was coconut scented; I liked that one because I could smear it on my nose and everything smelled tropical no matter what. I kept that one and tossed the rest. Are all the coolers necessary? Crackers and such don't need to be chilled. Tackle is necessary, but bringing the entire tackle store? How much rusted and corroded tackle have I tossed or wasted money on because I thought it necessary and pertinent to carry on every trip? Saltwater or salt air has ruined hundreds, if not thousands, of dollars per year before it was ever taken out of the package and used. That is real out-of-pocket money and was simply taking up space.

So I assessed everything on the boat on a has-to-stay or got-to-go basis. Lo and behold, I found my boat from under the clutter. In a moment of brilliance, I bought a large plastic container and set it empty inside the center console. It was designated space for other people's stuff. If what they brought didn't fit, then some of it had to be left behind. At first, folks griped, but by the next trip they had trimmed their necessary items back to fit in the container.

I'm on a roll. Here are a few more captain tips that will prove worthy to put a little more fun in the fishing day.

Recreational fishing is supposed to be relaxing. The thesaurus gives similar words for recreation such as fun, entertaining, and leisure, even frivolous. It is a shame we set special time aside for, spend hard earned money on, and invite special, loved people to join in on, then turn it around and pressurize the recreation so that folks don't want to do it again, because it wasn't the fun expected.

An ounce of prevention: Take a half hour or more to make sure the boat and tackle are in good working order; you don't want to wait until the boat ramp to find out the battery had died since the last time you took the boat out, corrosion knocked out an electronic or bilge pump, the grease set up like cement in your reels, your fishing line is as brittle as fried hair, your hooks or lures formed a chunk of modern art, your left over lunch or bait from the last trip is still waiting for you to open the box of mystic colors and odors or other unwanted surprises. No one is going to be happy if they went through all the motions to get there only to return home due to a preventable issue.

Proper attire: I had a young man show up dressed in a black hat, black long sleeve shirt, and black denim jeans three times his size, black socks and black shoes, and if I had to venture a guess as to the color of his drawers, I'd say black. He was making a fashion statement of some sort, but it was July in Florida! Before we left the dock, I took him aside and explained his clothes were going to make him very uncomfortable. He looked at me like I was very uncool. At eleven am I looked at him, and he was literally very uncool. Always bring appropriate layered cloths and light weight rain gear, because regardless of season, the weather changes over the course of a day, sometimes drastically, and you need to be prepared. The point is if you're sweating bullets or freezing your toes off, you are not comfortable. If you're not comfortable, it is impossible to have fun.

Know your limits—it has nothing to do with fish: If the weather is real bad, don't go! If the offshore conditions are poor, too much for your boat and/or abilities, don't go! If someone has the slightest thought that death is a real possibility today, they are not going to have fun fishing. Limits also apply to your crew. You might be willing to bound through a three-foot, hard chop for an hour and a half to have a shot at a grouper, but if the grand kids or grandma are riding with you today, sea bass and grunts are your ticket to happiness. If there is somebody new to the game onboard, five minutes of special attention at the beginning can eliminate a major backlash later in the day. If the crew is fresh to the offshore experience, then an elaborate trolling spread will only lead to the most complicated knot of lines ever seen on your boat, complete with some of the macramé wrapped around your prop. No one wants to feel like an idiot because they screwed up what appeared to be a simple task. There have been times when I felt like an idiot, and I've never been happy feeling that way. If you keep pushing people to do things on a boat they are not familiar with, and they screw it up once or more, they will feel bad. Bad is the opposite of fun. It is OK to push a little to teach something new, but in general, conform to the crews fishing level.

Teaching opportunities: Teaching is far more than barking, "Do that." Teaching means explaining with some show-n-tell. Most folks don't mind learning some things as they go along, for example, how to hook live bait without killing it. A good attitude and patience from the teacher will make most say "that's easy; let me try it." Learning something new adds fun to any experience. Yelling or showing anger makes things un-fun quick. If someone doesn't get the trick the first time, smile and take a free do-over.

Go with the flow: I've been traveling along and seen Spanish mackerel or bonito blowing up on bait pods. I turned the boat towards the fracas and that half hour to forty-five minutes turned out to be the most fun part of the entire day. If you happen to see an opportunity for fun, by all means take it. It is a gift. Don't let the pursuit of food rob you and others of a good time.

Scale down for fun: Grunts, the saving grace of many an offshore trip, are fun to catch. They are even more fun to catch if you do it with lightweight gear. The same principle applies using large, spinning tackle for kingfish, cobia, amberjack and even grouper. After all, if fish didn't fight back, we'd lose interest in catching them using hook and line. Putting more fight in the fish by using lighter tackle puts more fun in the fishing. Try it; you'll like it.

Keep the kids in mind: Imagine taking a kid bowling and forcing them to use the big sixteen-pound ball. The next time you ask them to go bowling, the kid is going to think about how much work it was and not want to play. Sticking a heavy bottom reel and rod in a little one's hands is great for a photo op but works them just to keep it steady in their small hands. A shorter, lighter weight combo would be more appropriate and bring fun in the game. Besides, children have the wonderful ability not to distinguish between fishes. There are no trash fish. If it wiggles and pulls, it is the best fish in the sea at the moment.

The Kodak pole: I can't count the number of times the best fish of the day came from using the Kodak pole. The Kodak pole produces the fish you want your picture taken with. The Kodak pole can overwhelm your boat in surprised excitement at any time. So what is this Kodak pole? An unattended pole with a free lined bait off the transom while you're busy bottom fishing. You may set it out many times without getting a sniff, but that one time when the line screams off towards the horizon and an over grown king, cobia, or grouper snatches it down, will make all the past efforts worthwhile. It has proven itself, over and

60

over, to be the pinnacle point of fun in a day of fishing.

Break up the boat ride: Long boat rides are boring. After you lose sight of the tree line, it all looks the same. Unless the crew can sleep, play cards, or entertain themselves for a while, riding more than an hour at a shot gets boring. I try and keep the boat rides to around forty-five minutes at the most. It keeps the boredom factor down. I like to do a fifteen-minute fishing stop. If the fish are there, great…you didn't run over a good time you would have otherwise missed out on. If the fish aren't there, settle in for another run, and do the same thing. Remember to try and do the same thing on the way in, or you're looking at a long ride home. This hopping offshore plays well with the variety fishing method. Fishing is the fun part; the ride is the necessity.

Music tames the savage beast: Satellite radio, marine stereo system, or a Walmart twenty dollar boom box adds music when things are happening hand over fish or when there happens to come a great lull in action. Bring some music that you and the others would enjoy hearing. I've had a tune come on that had me dancing around the deck like the first white man to find rhythm. Actually, some people thought I was trying to stomp on a roach, but I was having a moment of fun, and sometimes people joined me. Music is fun; bring it with you.

Listen to people: I've been offshore so much I forget that others may feel somewhat uncomfortable going so far away from land. They have strong concerns about the boat, the motors, the weather, the safety equipment, and the sanity of a captain they may have seen stomping invisible roaches on the deck. If someone is worried, he/she isn't going to have a bunch of fun. Be easy with him/her and don't make the first leg of the journey too long so they worry. Let him/her have enough time to become more comfortable with their new surroundings. If they tell you they don't want to go very far offshore, then keep it within them seeing the tree line. Sometimes it just takes a couple of stops before they're telling you to, "let it rip".

Do not ignore your obsession: Plan a trip for your level of fishing obsession with people as crazy about fishing as you are. You can't keep the horse in the barn all the time. Some trips aren't meant for those who don't want to grip and rip like you want to. If you are like me, I need a good day of hardcore fishing. I need to drop big baits to big fish and have them try and pull my arms out. I want to feel blown out when the line wraps the cleat at the dock.

Fishing is fun. Love it, and pass it on.

I hope my experienced advice serves you and your boat well. I've learned a bunch over time and dealing with various people. One thing I've learned to be adaptable to weather conditions, fishing conditions and, most importantly, people conditions.

And you can always accumulate a bunch of crap on a boat in a short amount of time. Now, if someone wants a pack of crackers, they have to disembark and go to the convenience store to pick up a stale dusty pack from the shelf; it's not on my boat!

The doer alone learneth.
Nietzsche

The Salt of a Woman

Of all the people I've taken fishing over the years, only ten to fifteen percent have been female, and that small portion has come wrapped in all types of packages. And like gifts at a White Elephant party, you never know what you're going to get.

Some just come up to the boat and step aboard like they are getting into a car—a car that is going to take them to the fish mall. They fish shop for the day, then ride back home. It's just another day of running around.

Some have to wrap their arms around me to help them get on the boat. The young ones who do that, I just pick up and lift over the side. Once released, they take off like they're entering a theme park. The older ones who do that embrace me and do the 'gunnel swing' dance where their rear is first eased onto the flat gunnel, her legs kick out flapper style, and we swing one hundred eighty degrees into the boat; then they plop down on the deck, and we waltz to the captain's bench.

The mothers have to be relieved of an armload of stuff before coming onboard. They must have three arms because it takes me three trips back and forth to empty them. Mothers are prepared to go to *Gilligan's Island*.

There are the quiet ones who appear to be on a forced fish march to make their significant other happy. They appear to have just eaten a sour apple, are earmarked with a motion sickness patch, rattle with Dramamine tablets in their pockets when they get on aboard and clutch a tube of SPF150 sunbeam annihilator cream. They don a Minnie Pearl style—price tag blowing in the wind—wide-brimmed hat just bought from the marina.

There are party girls who celebrate simply getting together by twisting off a wine cooler first thing in the morning. That usually includes a group photo taken by me, the captain. Sometimes, they request me in the photo as well. The mate takes the picture, or if they find the mate cute, I take the photo of them with him.

There are sun-tanned girls draped in their boyfriends' over-sized T-shirts wearing cut-off jeans with bikinis underneath. They bring a gigantic fashionable bag of towels and smell of coconut. They aren't going to fish.

There are teenage girls with knapsacks loaded with "stuff." If the mate is semi-cute, they fawn a little puppy love attention his way over the course of the day. If he starts to like the interest, I whisper to him "fish bait not jailbait," to bring him back to reality.

There are redneck gals out to prove they are just as tough as any man who ever fished offshore. Most are tougher or fake it for the day. I don't care which is true. Those Southern belles with pumped up hair, a little extra make-up, a mouth that lacks control, and clothes that are modestly snug, reveal they drink a couple beers just on the weekends, and they are just fine by me. I'm from the south. I love country women.

There are rich, pampered girls and women who come aboard and whose facial expression is like they just stepped foot on a Junk out of Hong Kong. We cater to all their needs, but I wait for them to ask the most common question.

Most of the ladies get onboard and wonder what the day will bring. Generally, the women have limited offshore experience…if any. They tend to be reserved. They notice where things like life jackets, fire extinguishers, coolers, and food are located. They notice if the boat is clean, the towels are clean, the mate is clean, and if I am clean. They wonder about all the fishing equipment.

"How many poles do we need to catch a stupid fish in the first place?"

"What are all these little plastic fish about?"

"Will I be expected to bait my own hook?" They wonder about living conditions over the next hours.

"Will I get cold, hot, wet, or feel in any way icky?" They mostly ignore all the electronic gizmos. They wonder about the goofy looking guy behind the steering wheel. "Are you the boat driver?"

"Yes ma'am, I'm the captain."

"Really?" I guess I don't look that bright. "How far out are we going?" When I answer they say, "That far…. Can we catch fish closer to land?"

"Don't worry," I reply. "I make it back to Steinhatchee nine out of ten times on average." Their look is priceless. When we approach the end of the no wake zone, I ask one or two of the most timid to come sit with me on the captain's bench. "It's the most comfortable seat on the boat...." As they come, I tell them I'm flirtatious.

The husbands or boyfriends laugh, sometimes the women do too, but I always get the *look*. All women are born with the *look*. Not all looks are the same, but every guy knows the look. If the look were lethal, there would be very few men left in the world; most survivors would have been born blind.

I could go on, but I don't want to even feel the look from lady readers. I'm sensitive.

The common question from the women is, "Where is the restroom?" A question guys never ask. I've had camper porta-potties secured inside the center console for private female discretionary needs. However, experience from previous foul incidents educated me that the nice, little, cheap plastic potties aren't built to handle offshore conditions. "I'll show you when you need it."

A five-gallon bucket is stalwart. A bucket has no plumbing to clog, no pump to fail, and I don't have to hand tote the gift off the boat at the end of the day. A job the CDC would require me to wear a haz-mat suit to perform safely. Though mate and I are exposed to a lot of "icky" over the course of our day, there are some things we don't want to slosh on ourselves. Simply dump the contents of the bucket overboard and the event is done. It is a natural function that requires no special attention. Don't make a big deal of it, and do it down wind. The majority of women understand, especially outdoor women, and accept it. The other women come to terms with it, given sufficient pressure.

One day I had Joe and his wife Shirley, Jimmy and his wife Wanda, and Jim and his wife Joyce. All were in their early forties. The guys were buds from high school times; they played ball together, knew each other's secrets, rooted in each other's lives like brothers, and chose fishing here and there over the years as an excuse to get together. The ladies were new to the fishing togetherness game. They were reserved, excited, and somewhat nervous. They asked the question. I confessed the truth. Collectively, they came to grips with the "dirty bucket." Twenty minutes after passing the last channel marker, we stopped to collect from the bait traps. The majority of the ladies liked this part. It must be a genetic draw to babies. The little fish flipped about, and they watched.

Sometimes we do a brief show and tell if they seem interested. From little girls to grandmothers, fish petting is a fun part of the morning. "This is a pinfish and that is a grass porgy. The one over there is a black seabass." We, one by one, go through the fish with the ladies. "Yes that one is pretty; it's a squirrelfish." While we do that the guys play off like they know it all, but when I glance past the ladies, I see that some of the guys taking notice. The ladies listen and learn, and then, it's offshore.

"It'll be about forty-five minutes to get to the fishing grounds. It won't be a bad ride out. Some of you can jump in the bean bags and take a nap."

Wanda was sitting beside me on the captain's bench. "So what's the biggest fish you ever caught Wanda?"

"Well, one time I caught a bass and…"

In the meantime, the guys were talking about who was going to catch the big one. I interrupted, "Guys, I got five bucks on Wanda." They smiled it off. They forget who was driving the boat and baiting the hooks.

Thirty minutes en route, I stopped short to bottom fish a warm up spot where there were a few grouper and a nest of hungry Florida snapper—grunts. There, Lil B, our mate and I showed the ladies how to hold the pole, how to feel the bite, and what to do when the fish is on. While we did that, the guys played off like they knew it all, but when I glanced past the ladies, I saw some guys taking notice. The ladies again listened and learned. It didn't take too many fish before the ladies were doing everything on their own. And they were not going through some macho, random, electro-shock therapy as they were reeling up a fish. The ladies became smooth, mostly in control. When a good fish was on, they weren't too proud to ask for help either.

We eased out to where I wanted to seriously bottom fish. The bite started fast and ended soon, so we moved on from one spot to the next, fish collecting. After a while, one of the guys noticed Wanda was slightly ahead in the keeper grouper category. The "grip and rip" technique was being out done by the "slow and steady" girly style. Late in the morning, I slipped in some trolling.

Trolling is a great way to catch grouper, kingfish, as well as other fish. I do it when spot A and B aren't that far from one another. That broken interlude allows the guests snack time and me to peek-a-boo, via sonar, at the bottom between two productive spots. If you find one good house of grouper, you may have found a neighborhood.

I'm always searching for new and exciting bottom. You can't make a living, much less a reputation, traveling the same route like a postman. I know I'm not Christopher Columbus discovering new ground. Fishing pressure offshore from Steinhatchee isn't that great, but I do consider the number of boats. Some fishermen aren't that skilled and are basically stumbling across fish blindly. Other fishermen bought the "package offshore deal" with electronics they don't fully understand how to use. Then there are the wealthy who purchase the top of the line everything bought to impress, but the electronic equipment manuals are as thick as a New York City telephone book. They usually don't have the time or the inclination to figure things out. But the old boats with antiquated electronics, helmed by old Salts who look like they are getting toward the last voyage, slip by the public eye unnoticed. They, most assured, have been to my new honey hole before me. Nonetheless, to me, fresh is best.

Women tend to like trolling because they enjoy a nice, slow-paced cruise. Trolling also levels the playing field for the ladies. The momentum on the boat sets the hook, quickly yanks the grouper away from the security of its own backyard, and often, due to the outsized lures—ten to fourteen inches—trolling is large fish selective.

Men tend to shy away from the trolling gig because they never experienced it. They don't believe it will catch grouper, and it's not the "grip and rip" reel monkey thing they thought was going to occur all day long. Guys tend to lack interest or faith; thus while trolling, they busy themselves swilling beer, and munching snacks. They sometimes occupy themselves by lighting up cigars to pass time while the boat slow moves through the water toward their next expectation.

"Fish on, fish on!" The port stern rod bucked flat out. "Folks clear the other trolling gear." The extra gear was cleared in a hurry.

The women politely ushered Wanda to the buck flat pole. Wanda remembered what the mate said, "All you have to do when the fish is on is ease the rod up, no yank, then reel quickly while dropping the rod down allowing no line slack."

Wanda did it perfectly? No. She struggled for every foot of monofilament. I reiterated in a whisper what Lil' B told her. She improved well. A fifteen-pound gag grouper was digitally caught on several cell phones before it hit the ice. That was the big one for the day, so far.

Once the big fish was put on ice, their hubbies suddenly wanted to participate in the trolling gig. It's funny how things work like that. They gathered interest, repented, and got faith.

The bottom fishing and the intermission trolling produced about one hundred pounds of grouper for the new, totally interested, mixed gender party. Everyone had his or her moment to shine. Not a bad haul considering the number of short grouper released and the harsh grouper regulations imposed.

At some time during the day, the boat was near an abundant amberjack haven. Folks got dipped in an amberjack acid test. Amberjack hit, pull, yank, dive, and make belly bruises better than any fish in the Gulf. They earned the nickname "reef donkey."

We got the boat anchored right. Wanda was jazzed on what had happened so far but naïve as to what was about to happen. I was concerned for her, because I knew what was about to happen. It was donkey time.

I pitched a frisky live bait out and attempted to explain what to do, but I was interrupted when the pole doubled over. Still talking, I handed her the pole. Lil' B dashed off to get a fighting belt.

"Oh, God," Wanda blurted out loud. "

Just be steady; let the drag and pole tire the fish,"

"Oh, my God!" She reblurted. It was funnier the second time.

Lil' B slapped the belt around her waist. I put the butt of the rod in the cup of the fighting belt. "You can do it, girlfriend!"

Sometimes ladies use colorful words in special moments. The guys saw and heard that and dug in to get their fill of grip and rip warfare. She brought in a thirty-pound fish after an eternal fifteen-minute epic battle. We high fived, hugged, and took a Kodak moment. And I stupidly thought she needed a break. Oh no, silly boy. She wanted another bait. Now!

I've seen many a guy sit down after dealing with two good amberjacks yet been amazed by women who stood against the gunnel to battle jack after jack until I was tired just helping them. They kept going and going and going…. If fishing were a professional sport, these women would need to be drug tested. That reserved woman who got on the boat a few hours ago was showing her salt. Men became embarrassed with their lackluster effort to keep up the pace.

Joe, Jimmy, and Jim macho-ed out after dealing with two fish each. They kicked back, popped a top, and debated whose fish was the biggest.

"We'll let the ladies have their fun."

"Right." They looked whipped.

The ladies never gave up! They did allow some individual rest between fish by dropping out then filing back in, one by one, helping each other, until the live bait finally ran out.

Funny, if a man is struggling, the other men will razz him as if he dropped the ball in the fourth quarter. Yet, if a woman is having some trouble, her girlfriends will rush to her aid, often before the mate or I realize the need. And when that occurs, they turn in unison and give one or both of us a united *look*. "Aren't you going to do something about this?"

We're guys too. We can't mind read chick.

The limit for amberjack is one per person—does not include the captain and crew. That day, we could have a total of six. I had whispered to Lil' B, "Just toss five in the fish box."

I had a trick to put an XL donkey in the box. I snuck back to the helm and tied on an eleven-inch topwater plug to a large, spinning combination. I refer to the large topwater plug as a "sorter" because smaller fish may slap at it, but it takes a big fish to win it. I double-checked the drag on the reel. The plug was expensive.

Lil' B lied, telling the ladies we were out of bait. Joyce, in a high voice, said, "Out of bait!"

"Joyce, I've got something for you," I responded in expectation. I showed her the setup and explained, after casting it way out and letting the plug lay still. "All you have to do is quick short-snaps to pop the lure and continue to short-snap and pop, never stopping until you feel the weight of the fish on the line. Never stop moving the lure, ever," I made clear.

By then, the donkeys were so jacked up, this was going to be a one-shot shop. I handed her the pole. She started. I told her quicker but not to pull the lure so far across the top of the water while doing so. Women listen. Within fifteen feet, the chase was on. She paused.

"Remember, don't slow down," I said emphatically. She kept the plug moving like it was a small live fish being bum rushed by a hoard of hungry large fish. And then, an alpha amberjack arched from behind the crowd, mouth open, and engulfed the plug. The rod doubled down. The drag squealed.

Joyce colored her language. Lil' B strapped a belt around her. And the guys, knowing they were well behind, realized this was like first and goal with the ball on the one-yard line for their loved opponents, seconds to play, and they couldn't defend against the impeding score. They were gentlemen sportsmen and cheered for Joyce. After twenty minutes, she slid a thirty-nine-pound donkey into the net, a quality fish for our neck of the woods. The big fish of the day!

So why are women good so consistently? One, the women listen and pay attention. The mate and captain have been there before. If they are good and honest, the advice given is valid. If for no other reason than the more fish caught, the happier you are, and the better they look at the end of the day. Two, women don't try to over muscle the fish but let the tackle do the work. Believe it or not, women are better kingfish and cobia fishermen than men because they aren't trying to rip the hook from the fish's mouth during the course of battle. They slowly and steadily wear the fish down. Last year, a lady brought a sixty-eight-pound cobia to the boat in less than five minutes. The fish didn't even know it was hooked. It came to the boat like a called dog. The next week, a man took over forty minutes to boat a forty-eight pound cobia that thought it was being yanked to the moon.

Most importantly, women are there to have fun. They don't put themselves in some stupid contest. Fishing is supposed to be fun. They get it. I mentioned at the beginning that women come in all types of packages from the small to large, and they have all proven to be fun.

Ladies don't let the thought of a five-gallon open potty deter you from a good time on the Gulf. Honestly, that bucket beats a cramped, smelly, dank head—boat restroom—any day. I watch every man onboard during your necessary time. I've never seen a man, even the rough ones, not be a gentleman—though I did have to give one the 'look'. He was old and forgetful; that is how he explained his action to me at least.

The clearest sign of wisdom is continued cheerfulness.
Montaigne

The Preacher Finally Gets It

Yesterday, I was down on the docks, disappointing six guys. Denver, Tommy, Michael, Derek, Matt, and Preacher David from North Georgia were supposed to be going fishing, but a cold front had recently passed over making the wind pump strong from the north. We were talking in a place where our northern exposure was well blocked, so it felt too pleasant for the forecast to be true. Yet at the mouth of the Steinhatchee River, the north winds blew all back to reality and all of us could see the "elephants dancing" on the horizon.

I felt bad about the situation, but good, because I saved them their money, as well as, an all-day, cold, wet, body beating. The high point was they were scheduled to fish the next day as well, and the forecast was the best seen in weeks. I left them with good thoughts for tomorrow.

The next morning was so cold there was ice on the boat! No, I'm not talking about ice in bags to chill fish or drinks but a thin film covering the fiberglass. I bent over and looked at it as if looking at some artifact in a museum case. I tapped it with my knuckles and verified it as the genuine article...ice. This was Florida, well, North Florida.

Should we spray water on it? Would that make it go away? Or, worse, make it grow thicker like fertilizing grass? It was a quandary for me. I lollygagged around the dock an extra half hour thinking about it, basically avoiding the cold. The rising sun softened the ice and allowed it to slough off the boat. That proved the point—given enough time, problems often solve themselves.

We shoved off thirty-two minutes late, but ice-free. My boat is a thirty-two-foot by twelve open Twin Vee catamaran. The spaciousness, useable fishing room, makes it a wonderful fishing platform, yet roll-down, plastic curtains don't completely block the chill. Appropriate layered garb is necessary. Under normal circumstances, the benefit of space far outweighs the need to dress for conditions. Then again, cabins and enclosures can lead folks to not bother with appropriate apparel, so they find themselves uncomfortable doing what they planned on doing, fishing. I've found layered clothing the best call for many applications and a water or wind proof outer layer the most important. Think about it...unrestrained square miles of water surround you. You might happen to get damp or soaking wet, then cold to the bone. "Be Prepared," like the Boy Scout motto.

The wind was from the east, seas one to two foot and slowly building the further west we traveled. It made the six-mile ride to the bait reef easy, yet made me uneasy. Home, on Florida's left coast, is west. Sustained east winds can make the journey home lumpy, if the wind doesn't lay or change directions. We'd have to deal with what blew our way this day. The forecast was for conditions to ease up, but I'd rather have a weather bookie than a professional meteorologist. I read the clouds. Their absence told me, as the air temperature rose to equilibrate with the sea temperature, conditions would improve. I was banking on it to occur as soon as possible.

Bait fishing went quick. Some guys were bringing squirrel fish, porgies, lizardfish, pinfish, and occasional cigar minnows aboard as fast as they could unpin the hook. A couple of dudes struggled to do the same, which forced our collective decision for compassion or mockery. We all went directly to mockery. Boys never fully mature.

Sixty some live baits later, approximately forty minutes, we headed to battle the amberjacks. The further west we traveled, the higher the east winds pushed the seas, up to two to four foot, occasionally larger. The catamaran ride gave us the motion of the ocean but no slam body payments. The sea conditions made the first anchor deposit a bust; however, the second chance set us on the action.

Actually, the action swam up to the boat! "There they are," I said coming around the helm station. That told everyone to look overboard.

"Would you look at that?" and more comments came as the crew witnessed hordes of AJs swim under the boat.

Jake, our trusty mate got busy setting out two free-liners off the stern and two weighted baits amidships. I slipped a large spinner combo from the top rod rack. While they were live bait fishing, I tied on a Creek Chub 6 Pin popper I had removed the two original factory treble hooks from and replaced them with a large single hook to the end of the plug. One could fly that plug in the stiffest of winds. I flung it over the crew. It landed well out in the swells. No one noticed because two guys were being bent in half by amberjacks. I worked the top water popper back to the boat hard and fast. Water foamed with each jerk and twitch. The men took notice of the plug when one amberjack ambushed it about twenty yards from the boat. That fish missed, but the one coming from underneath didn't. The drag squealed a high pitched "fish on."

I didn't have to say it but did it anyway "Fish on!" The first guy I looked at, Tommy had a total face gimme look; I handed him the pole. He was a diehard-bass fisherman who loved top-water fishing. However, this wasn't a scrappy bass doing a brief yet exciting top-water dance as you sat in a cushioned-pedestal bow chair. This was a twenty-some-pound amberjack built for speed, muscled for endurance, and obviously pissed off. Tommy fought with knees bent and back hunched over.

I walked over to Derek doing a big "reef donkey," using a 4/0 and bottom rod. I whispered, "What you are experiencing at this very moment is your arms being pulled from your shoulders and your back being stretched an inch while your fingers cramp." He made a grimaced face noise.

This was a constant happening for an hour and a half. Why did it take so long to load up six amberjack? Well, some of the battles, some long and some short, ended in broken lines, straightened-out hooks, or lost fish. It does take time to re-rig, and honestly, the guys needed breaks between fish. We were enjoying the fellowship.

Also, during that time, Michael yakked but came back for more. Gina, my wife, noted that Michael would be fishing inshore the first day yet might not be going offshore the next. He was prone to motion sickness, but with the first day cancelled due to weather, he opted to join in on the offshore day. He pushed himself through the amberjack experience, but succumbed to the comfort of the beanbag the remainder of the day. Michael was with us in spirit not body, quite the trooper.

The ride to the grouper grounds took twenty minutes. The guys needed the rest and ate lunch. The grouper bite was steady. Most of the grouper were a fraction of an inch short. It didn't matter. The short grouper and large Florida snapper kept the action up. The action was punctuated when someone hooked up a good keeper gag or red grouper. Many of the keepers that were hooked got off. Nonetheless, enough made it over the gunnels to make a good mess.

Unfortunately, all of Preacher David's keepers managed to escape the cooler. I watched him and could tell by the flex of his pole, the fish he had were quality. I also noticed, when he yanked the rod up to set the hook, he would immediately drop it back down, creating slack in the line. The fish took that opportunity to escape. I went over to coach him a bit, but he turned to me and quoted my thoughts.

"You know the problem," I said. Bad habits are hard to break. However, in the last five minutes of our day, his line was pulled down—a prayer line went up as well—and a two-foot gag grouper made the box. We knuckle bumped.

He said, "Praise the Lord," in a Pentecostal tone. Hallelujah!

Hallelujah too, the weather and seas calmed down for the ride home. Michael managed to get up out of the beanbag to let some fresh air clear his head.

You won't catch every fish you try for, but don't let that discourage you because the best fishermen who ever lived can't do it either.
H. G. Tapply

King of the Late Afternoon

The river was flat calm, but as we passed Lazy Island, at the mouth of Steinhatchee River, a northeast breeze had the Gulf in a one to two foot chop. The chop bumped up to two to three feet once five miles off Steinhatchee #1. The Twin Vee catamaran cut through the waves as if they weren't there. The day was pleasant and expected to "pretty-off." The only downside was the morning chop kept bait pods down. I planned to do some mackerel, mainly king, fishing on the way out. However, with the bait down, I wasn't going to fish a blind surface.

So I pulled up on a piece of bottom that normally held blue runners and other quality baitfish. In forty-five minutes, we put eight blue runners—Midas bait—and a couple dozen mix of squirrelfish, genuine pinfish, grass porgies, and spot tailed pinfish in the tank. It was a good start. We had two boxes of frozen threadfin and five pounds of squid as backup fish food.

I held back using the blue runners during the day. Most of the other live bait was donated to amberjack. The little wigglers produced a base catch of four, eighteen-to-twenty-pound reef donkeys. We hit those on the way out to the grouper. The remainders of the live bait, excluding the runners, were dropped down to produce five, nice red grouper. We also caught a limit of fine gag grouper we were required to toss back because of a stupid law written by the politically uninformed soft-hands-minds that never endured hardship earning their dollar at sea.

The average gag grouper weighed ten pounds. According to the Federal government, gag grouper are near extinction. So, accordingly— "trying to be facetious"—we were catching the last of the Mohicans. Statistically, what Big Brother is saying, verses what we did in a three-hour period, doesn't jive. If the gag grouper fishery was in such bad shape, we would have been hard-pressed to catch a single one, much less feel the need to move off a piece of bottom because of their nuisance-abundance for fear of harming a fish we can't harvest. We did kill one gag that horribly swallowed the circle hook. We cut the line at the mouth, but she still floated away. What a waste! I could get on my soapbox about it, but I'd just be preaching to the choir.

During some miscellaneous Florida snapper and black fishing, we picked up ten more random blue runners. All but one went in the livewell. The one that was dropped to the bottom attracted the attention of a fifteen-pound "extinct" gag grouper. By that time I was so ticked off at the nonsense regulation, it would have been easier to toss the rod and reel over than the fish!

After two o'clock, the seas went slick. The baitfish pods would be on the surface. My thoughts were on those seventeen blue runners swimming circles in the livewell. With high hopes of ending the day with an exclamation-point smoker king, I asked everyone to reel in and get comfortable for a forty-five minute quick cruise east, shoreward. When we were within fifteen miles of the coast, I peeked over the windshield and scanned side to side and looked for dimples on the water. If I didn't see bait pods, I had put myself in a pickle. I bet a good chunk of the fishing trip on finding baitfish on the surface. No guts, no glory, and confidence is always the best bait.

I did a double take when I first saw the shaky water. Yes! Bait! I eased the motors into neutral, the boat slid to stop, and I cut the motors off. My mate, Casey, and I quickly put together three king poles. The process went fairly fast as I had pre-made, wire kingfish rigs. One rig was weighted to keep the bait near the bottom and close to the boat at amidships on windward side. The other two were heavy, spinning tackle with floats, one set near the surface and the other set and weighted at twelve feet. One was to be tossed off the stern and the other off the bow, windward.

After watching the movement of the bait pods and considering the motion of the wind and sea, I positioned the boat and set the runners out on their wire bridles. To the best of my ability, I wanted us to blend quietly into the waters with the pod. I cut the sonar off. My guess turned out pretty good.

Just outside of the pod perimeter, the spinning rod, with the runner set at twelve feet, squealed drag so intensely, I thought I'd turn to see a puddle of molten metal instead of a reel. Half the line was gone before Fred could grab it. He was standing next to the reel!

"Reel in the other lines!" I screamed over the sound of the happening. The guys scrambled to do it as I kicked the motors over. Fred was having difficulty getting the rod from the holder as I was twisting the wheel in the direction of the bolt off the bow. But once I was able to put the boat in hot idle, Fred was able to pull the rod free. The other two baits came over the gunnel about the same time. Casey picked the spare runners off their riggings, tossed them in the tank, and stowed the rods neatly in the rocket launcher behind the captain's bench. Now, it was all about Fred.

I eased the throttles back to slow idle while verbalizing Prozac to Fred, just to calm him down. He was going into Jack Russell mode, and I wanted him to be a Bassett hound at the moment. Casey was up on the starboard bow also giving Fred sedative suggestions.

More kingfish are long line released by over-zealous anglers than get away by their own misbehaved cunningness. Unless you've been there, a hyper fish moment will trick one into a hyper response. However, just like in any other hyper-emergency moment, a cool, collective response is best.

We were negotiating Fred into catching the kingfish, moment by intense moment. The two large beanbags were tossed over the coolers and forward helm seat to allow Fred to easily move around the entire boat. Nonetheless, I kept the boat so the battle would remain off the starboard and move to the stern. The kingfish was juking to and fro, making necessary boat adjustment quick to maintain what I wanted.

Multiple times the fish approached the boat only to dash away. Once, while near the boat, the king ditched under the stern forcing a motor shut down and fast dual up tilt. With Casey forcing Fred to plunge half the rod in the water, the line cleared. When the fish darted away, I dropped the motors back in the water to resume positioning.

Each run became less dramatic. Each run stopped closer to the boat. We had seen the fish on a couple of occasions. My take was a fish pushing forty pounds. The main hook was lodged in the corner of the mouth. The stinger hook was stuck in the flesh on top of the head. The hooks seemed secure, but you never know. Strange things happen in the blink of a tail swing.

Casey has worked with me since he was thirteen and has gaffed more fish than most weekenders ever will. However, do I wage a quality fish in the hands of a seventeen year old? If I take the gaff, I embarrass him and show lack of trust to the crew. If I don't take the gaff, and we lose the fish, the crew will doubt his abilities because of his youth and question me.

I bet on Casey at the bat, yet I got the second gaff ready. When the fish passed by the rail the second time, Casey whacked it behind the gill plate. He groaned when experiencing the total weight of the fish out of the water. The king was heavy in air. I snatched the bottom of the gaff and helped roll it over the gunnel and dropped back behind the helm. He was humble in the limelight. Fred fist bumped Casey. The rest of the guys went for cameras. A few minutes of clicks and the fish went in the fish box. It was a cool event.

We picked up one more king; it was a snake, small. We also picked up two more "extinct" gag grouper on runners set near the bottom before calling it a day.

Some people say they don't like eating kingfish. They have more than likely been served frozen kingfish. Kingfish should only be served fresh, never frozen!

Here is a simple recipe for fresh kingfish steaks:
Mix together half and half melted butter and soy sauce
Place the steaks in the mix for twenty minutes
Pull steaks, sprinkle with sesame seeds
Put steaks on smoking hot grill; about one and half minute per side
Apply fresh cracked black pepper, no salt

Good served over a bed of rice as it sops up the sauce.

I know of no optimism as great as that, which perennially blooms in the heart of a fisherman.
Burton L. Spiller

Some Like It Hot

It was close to middle July in Steinhatchee, Florida. The Mid-west on southward was experiencing higher than normal summer heat with no rain. On the boat, I've watched more water run down my legs than would flow from a trickle irrigation system at a nursery in the same amount of time. It was summertime in Florida; what would you expect? I wasn't looking forward to August, the hottest month.

***

One day after the next charter, I was dreaming of flopping in the closest pool to absorb water until I got kicked out. "Hey, there's a manatee in the pool wearing blue shorts, a Columbia shirt, and sunglasses, drinking a Diet Coke," a guest complained.

"Sir, you have to leave, or we're calling the deputy," said the manager.

"OK, I'll see you tomorrow about the same time," I said with a refreshed dripping grin as I walked away. He was lucky I didn't have enough time to break out the soap and washrag to leave a ring-around-the-pool during my unauthorized dip.

***

A damp mop of moist heat wrapped me the moment I stepped out of my air-conditioned house to ride down to the marina. I wouldn't call it breathing, rather sucking air through a steam towel. In the few minutes it took to get ready to ride to the marina, sweat rolled down the side of my face and under my arms. The heat was already a noose that would tighten as the sun rose high. By the time the boat was dressed up ready to go Jakes—our mat—and my clothes were wet from the inside out. We lingered in the air conditioning of the ship store as long as possible before diving in to the humidity outside when the folks showed up.

During our time in the store, I kept glimpsing at their Doppler radar. Yellow and orange popcorn storms were developing well enough to tie-dye the screen; most would dissolve while some would join together to make red, denoting lightning. However, they were spread apart enough so that I might slalom us through them. Furthermore, rain was spilling out of the strong systems; those well offshore telling me storm energy was dissipating as quickly and heavily as the water fell away.

Caution was still necessary, but there would be safe passage as the air temperature increased allowing the atmosphere to suck up more water vapor. The removal of humidity would save the now, yet make the evening storms extra intense.

An offshore angler becomes a forced meteorologist in time. By the way, it doesn't take long to determine the real meteorologists are as accurate as an egg-shaped cue ball. I don't know the difference between a forecast and an outright lie. I resort to reading clouds, isobars, radar, and sea buoy data to come to my own weather prognostication—a best guess developed from bad experiences.

By the time we were twenty-five nautical miles offshore, the dark clouds that were on the horizon had vanished into blue sky. The Gulf of Mexico was farm pond flat. The only thing that kept us from bursting into a full body sweat was the wind generated by the movement of the boat.

When the seas are most conducive for travel, the fishing is most "unconducive." There is no energy in the water making the fish lazy and aimless. Furthermore, divers have told me there were a "blue-zillion" baitfish carpeting the bottom, whether the bottom was sand, rock, flat, or broken in large chunks. A grouper could literally inhale and have lunch. I felt we were traveling to a great waypoint only to void into a rotary oscillator.

In the summertime, depth can help with the problem of lack of bite due to hot seawater. The deeper the water, the cooler it is at the bottom. In the Steinhatchee area, eighty to one hundred feet is considered deep and is located forty-five to sixty nautical miles offshore. It is a gamble to go that distance on a day trip, knowing severe thunderstorms are the odds upon return. It is best to take the long haul early and then jaunt

80

closer to "the hill" to be able to run in quick, not being caught long-term in the rough conditions of an electrical storm. A helpful hint: listen to your little voice that says go, not the one that says, "Ten more minutes." The voice saying ten more minutes has horns and deceives.

Anchoring wasn't necessary; the sea was slack. We saved a lot of time not dealing with the anchor. Jake was happiest of all of us. We dropped four Sabiki rigs on a piece of good bottom to reel up chains of Spanish sardines, cigar minnows, scad mackerel, and other live baits. It didn't take long to fill the livewell with prime bait. In the bait cooler were strips of squid wings and a five-pound box of threadfin herring, back up bait.

We rode another twenty-some minutes to settle on a section of flat bottom that showed hard, Swiss cheese-holed lime rock on sonar. According to the sonar image, the bottom was cluttered with bait. Our baits became one of countless, yet the only ones dealing with the handicap actions of a hook.

On the first three drops, we caught short red grouper after short red grouper and two whose tail squeezed above the twenty-inch minimum limit. I went on to a piece of bottom that had relief and added two free-lined baits to the presentation. Three mango snapper and one red snapper took the hapless wonders amongst short red grouper off the bottom. And then, the heat of the day spiked, coinciding with slack tide. There was no bite. Everybody endured forty-five minutes of sweating, holding a fishing rod from spot to spot.

It was time for a cool change. I pointed the boat towards Steinhatchee in an unhurried cruise letting the breeze bring us life. We headed toward "Gruntville" where the Florida snapper would make us forget about the heat, and from there; the ride back to Steinhatchee wouldn't be so long. I thought about the thunderstorms as well.

Cruising along, I noticed something that appeared to be a turtle about one o'clock. I steered toward it. Turtles reveal secrets, if asked politely. As we got closer, the supposed turtle was a drifting wooden pallet. I veered away before getting too close.

I asked Jake to gather the four trout combo's we use to collect bait off the forward rack. Everyone else was waking up when the motors throttled down. Beanbags are fine sleep makers. Together, we tied on eighteen inches of twenty-five pound test leader to the twelve pound mainline. Two leaders, Jake tied on a straight 3/0 hook and adorned one with an appropriate sized squid head and the other with the head

81

section of a diagonally cut dead cigar minnow. I tied on a green and yellow Mylar jig to the other two poles.

I gave the spiel of how and where to cast to the four anglers as I idled the boat toward and downstream of the flotsam. When we were close, they exclaimed what I thought was there. Dolphin! There was six or eight chicken dolphin flowing with the debris. We don't get the bull or cow dolphin here, but those chickens sure are fun to catch, and they dress a salad so nice. The "quad-cast" hooked us up into a four-fish dance on the bow. A spirited duck and twist around session resulted in two double dips of electrified fish. The last two jumped and flipped like the first four. It was over before we were ready for it to be. Nonetheless, it was a flash of fun to our day.

We resumed our ride to the hill. Folks slumbered in the hammock roll of the Twin Vee ride. I, on the other hand, was trying to stay awake like a long-haul trucker. Eighteen miles from the 1# marker Steinhatchee, we stopped to do a "pork chop" harvest. The live bottom held an abundance of one to three pound Florida snapper. In an hour, approximately one hundred pounds of sweet fillets graced the ice. Jake's and my hands were pincushions afterwards from quick mass handling. Florida snapper don't bring reputation to the dock, but the fillets rock the dinner table.

I'll testify the Florida snapper—white grunt—is the most under-rated yet one of the best eating fish the Gulf produces. Give me some fried grunt and whatever sides, and I'm in hog heaven.

For me, the day was a surprising success. The catch was far from the morning's expectations, but a part of fishing is going with the natural flow and discovering some unexpected surprises. Doesn't that seem like life? There is no menu; go with it.

See nature, and through her, God.
Henry David Thoreau

Trick Fished a Life Lesson

I was invited. I was invited! I was alone yumping and yumping. Yumping is a happy mixture of jumping while nerdishly flailing in a dysfunctional dance motion. It is an action or reaction that should only be performed while alone. Don't let others know you're a yumper. Even hardcore yumpers keep it a secret until they're accidentally caught yumping. Most likely you don't know me, so I'll confess, I'm yumping right now, remembering it again!

Two elderly gentlemen invited me to go fishing with them. I considered both these men my grandfather, though not by blood. Each one was involved in the foundation of our church, and I'm talking about putting the first blocks and brick down, as well as constructing the first school in the county. They had hunted and fished every acre of the county, worked and retired locally, and at some time served on every community board. The two were well recognized and respected. Each knew the family tree and felony record of just about anybody they ran across.

And I, at fourteen years old, was going fishing with Mr. Mac and Mr. Al on the first day after the full moon in March. Mr. Mac and Mr. Al had been fishing around here for so long they actually had fishing holes named after them. Those who incidentally happened upon Mr. Mac and Mr. Al fishing together or separate, labeled those holes. Those who intentionally followed the two men and spied them out garnered some of the spots clandestinely. Anyhow, if a fishing hole carried the name Mac and/or Al, people wanted to fish there. Mr. Mac and Mr. Al were so reliable, the family or church would pre-plan the fish fry days before they went on a fishing trip.

I don't yump for any occasion, but this occasion was indeed special enough for yumping. When Mr. Mac asked me to go, I immediately said, "Yes sir." In this situation, I didn't worry that Dad wouldn't let me set off with them. Just before my mind floated off, I remember Mr. Mac and Mr. Al saying something about sheep. I thought they'd have to do something with some flock before fishing so there would be a late start.

A couple days before the trip, Mr. Al called Dad and summed things up. After hanging up, Dad briefed me in his typical military style. "Son, Mr. Mac and Mr. Al are taking you sheepshead fishing on what is supposed to be the very best day of the year for catching sheepshead. Mr. Mac and Mr. Al are fine men, but they don't take too many folks fishing with them. I don't know how you pulled this off, how you got so lucky, but be on your best behavior. You clean the boat and all the fish, and don't run your mouth all day. As a matter of fact, keep your mouth shut unless they ask you to do something. And don't tell anybody but me where ya'll went," he smiled, saying the last part. Before walking off, he said, "Don't even tell me where they took you; we don't steal." I smiled back at him.

The night before the trip I couldn't sleep. I had so much energy running through me; I could have sold some back to the electric company. Through the rolling and turning, the flipping and flopping, and the anticipation dreams, I was surprised my alarm was necessary.

Mr. Al had the boat hooked up to his truck when he and Mr. Mac picked me up. I straddled the gear shifter between them as they talked to me about fishing; then they switched to farming and gardening, and I woke-up leaning on Mr. Mac when we got to the boat ramp.

Launching the boat was a routine matter for them. Nonetheless, enforced with Dad's previous chat, I got in the way as much as I could.

The boat was a well-used Ski Barge hull marked in rust and corrosion with scattered fiberglass Band-Aids yet set-up so fishing efficient, pro-boat manufacturers would have profited much if they had the opportunity or time to take a gander at this homegrown, redneck engineered boat appropriately named *Fish Trap*.

Fish Trap was powered by a thirty-five or maybe fifty hp tiller controlled motor with an after-market—off a lawn mower—electric starter. The motor cowling was a fiberglass patch quilt with some duct tape mixed in, a Jacob's robe of many colors, spray painted here and there for duck hunting. The motor was not decaled by brand or number. It was referred to as the "Whatchabang 100%" and always brought the men back home.

The ramp was a tide dependent, slightly inclined sandy spot on the estuary edge historically used to launch mullet net boats. The area crawled with fiddler crabs. Prior to the boat going in the water, Mr. Mac gave me a plastic bowl and said, "Go catch some of those crabs and put them in this cooler." He lifted the lid from the small cooler to show me where to put my catch. The cooler just had a wet towel in the bottom of it. It was a ploy to keep me busy, out of their hair.

While I scampered around the marsh trying to snatch crabs, Mr. Mac & Al took a shovel, dug a hole, lined it with a plastic sheet, and sanded down the edges. Then they started dancing circles around the sheet of plastic while clapping hands, hollering, and stomping the ground. I thought they had got caught up in the Pentecostal Spirit until one yelled, "go." On go, one ran to one end and the other to the other end of the plastic and snatched it off the ground while folding it in half. There were countless fiddler crabs scurrying on the plastic sheet when they took it up. They walked together to the bait cooler, dumped their load, and told me to get in the boat.

After witnessing the fiddler crab rodeo, I realized I wasn't much help. I grasped in my mind they didn't need any of my help. I really wasn't necessary in this deal.

I sat on the bow of *Fish Trap* looking aft in the direction of Mr. Mac riding amidships and then on back to Mr. Al running the "Whatchabang 100%" on the stern. The morning air was still cool. The misty bow spray was slowly working its way through my clothes and chilling me. We were ten minutes into a thirty-minute boat ride when I decided it was best for me to hunker down on the deck below the bow platform to avoid the mist. Mr. Mac had on a rain slicker ready for the mist.

I couldn't help myself from popping up every now and then for a peek forward. "Look for a big marker post off the bow," Mr. Mac told me. We were headed for open water; why would there be anything in front of us? Ten minutes later, "Do you see it?" It took me a while before I could make out a small, dark, vertical object on the horizon.

We'll be there in just a minute, I thought. I hunkered down to endure another hundred thousand plus bow slaps…that taught me, it is hard to judge distance over water.

When Mr. Al slowed the "Whatchabang 100%" down to idle, I popped up to see a huge Christmas tree structure made of steel I beams with a green billboard on top. The birds resting there obviously weren't happy with our arrival. They screeched off, leaving a fresh shot of the white paint to run down wherever it landed, steel or water.

Mr. Mac was busy getting the anchor ready as Mr. Al considered the direction the water was flowing by looking at rivets passing through the I-beams. The anchor was a huge and heavy double-fluted, rusted, handmade piece of blacksmith art attached to an eight-foot section of rusty chain that used to belong on a tractor. Upstream from the marker, Mr. Al said, "OK."

Mr. Mac placed the anchor in the water and played out rope. They worked as one. Mr. Al said, "OK," again, and Mr. Mac whipped the rope to the center bow cleat. The boat came to a solid stop twelve to fifteen feet ahead of the marker.

They were busy getting fishing gear in order. I was looking into the water. It was gin clear to the bottom. My eyes followed the marker I beams to the bottom. The marker was crawling from base to near surface with fish! It was a full-blown fish show. I'd never seen anything like it!

"Hey, ya'll see all those...." I stopped myself short, realizing these two men didn't just stumble across this spot. They drove directly to it, on a specific day with one select-bait, fiddler crab; my announcement wasn't going to be the grand surprise I first thought. I shut my mouth, as Dad told me.

The fishing tackle was simple spinning gear. The rig was a "knocker" where a quarter, three-eighths, or half ounce egg sinker, depending on tide strength, was slid on, followed by tying on a terminal long shank 1/0 hook. They then pierced the hook through the back leg joint of the fiddler crab and pushed it back out the top body trying not to kill the crab in the process. If the crab died during the process, it didn't really matter. It was probably better for the crab in the long run. The crab didn't have to sense...after all it'd been through today, the feeling of being eaten alive'.

The fishing was catching. Any crab that went down never returned. Many of the baits were stolen straight off the hook as we watched. It was as if being picked out by a magician while the audience observed him stealing your watch, wallet, and underwear, and you were standing there smiling and laughing with them.

Many fish fell for the fiddler crab bait and ended up in the fish-box. The box was quickly filling up. Some of the big fish required a net to bring them aboard; I was the happy-handy net-boy. Frequently, I'd net a fish for one of the gents, and they'd unhook it and flip it back in the water. When that happened, I shut my mouth as Dad told me.

In that day there were so few fishing regulations there was essentially "no law." I didn't know that at the time. I hooked the biggest sheepshead of my life. Mr. Mac netted it for me. While unhooking my best catch ever, I was all mouth. To me, it was the biggest fish caught that day. I showed the fish out, once unhooked.

Mr. Al, after enough listening said, "Quit yapping and let her go."

I pretended not to hear him as I moved toward the fish box. Mr. Mac repeated the same thing but louder. I coughed as I accidentally, maybe intentionally flopped the fish back. That hurt. I no longer was the happy-handy net-boy, just the net-boy.

It didn't take too long for the fish box to fill. I, the John Henry, had tried my best to keep up with the two machines, but they out fished me hands down. When the fish box was full enough, the remainder of the fiddler crabs were sacrificed to fish we left behind.

I cleaned the boat up. It was going to take a good long time to clean all the fish. I was happy Mr. Mac and Mr. Al pitched in and showed me how to do it faster and better.

It has been decades since that fishing trip. The marker is long gone. Both Mr. Mac and Mr. Al have gone to be with the Lord. Obviously, I remember that fishing trip well, but more importantly, I've had enough time to figure out why they were tossing back the biggest fish. They were releasing the big, fat, egg-laden females for forthcoming generations, for me. The fishing trip wasn't about them. It was a show for me. Now, I and others are catching the offspring of the fish Mr. Mac and Mr. Al gave back to us long ago. I'm thankful for them and others of the same ilk for their common sense and self-control. If each of us could exercise such self-control, there would be no need for external control over any of us.

If cats would use credit cards and cell phones, they could be herded.
Off the Grid

87

Seeing Red

At first light, I saw their eyes. They were Mars red, side-by-side, blank orbs punctuating drained faces. They'd gone out the night before fishing, fishing at our local watering hole bar and had lingered too long in the intoxicating atmosphere. Those who have prolonged exposure in that strange environment tend to develop morning headaches, sour stomachs, reduced motor abilities, retarded mental function, and other maladies. Sometimes the effects are so severe they don't make it to the boat at all early the next morning. It's best to save that "good time" after going fishing for fish. In their defense, these men did pony-up enough to make it to the dock. However, from the looks of a couple of guys, it was going to be like a mechanic working with a rubber screwdriver.

The meteorologist, weather "predicktors," stated that the seas were going to be two to four feet and building to six, as a cold front passed overhead. In the Gulf of Mexico the bottom is shallow; therefore, the waves become very steep suddenly, and boating becomes quite uncomfortable as well as dangerous, quickly. The adage, "Use your head, and fish tomorrow," holds value here. Although Florida right-hand, East-coasters may push the "go" button at six-footers or so, the left-hand sea is a much different animal.

I planned my day by the NOAA forecast; it is a legal document. We were punching out in the morning during the supposed smoother seas, then fishing back toward shore when the weather was presumed to deteriorate. My order of business is safety, fun, and fish. The order never changes, regardless of desire. The value of a big or desired fish is zero measured against anyone's health, safety, or life, every day with me.

Anyway, after collecting bait, the seas were doable, and I punched in an amberjack hole on my GPS. It was going to be the most distant point of the day. After that, I planned to fish back towards land.

The amberjacks were ready to party when we arrived. Live bait, whether free-lined or sunk down on lightweights suspended just above the bottom was sucked up by legal, as well as short AJs. For an hour, amberjack hammered hangovers. Much mojo was extracted during individual battles. Men flopped on the beanbags after their tour of duty at "Reef-donkey Ridge."

Florida snapper were the revival, for a while. The rapid bite of Florida snapper didn't allow time for them to feel how bad they felt. Six men, spending an hour banging out, a hundred pounds of delicious eats, brought life back to the boat. And then there was a secondary beanbag crash.

Trolling was mandatory to allow for rest and rehabilitation. My mate, Jake, and I set out the trolling spread ourselves. It wasn't worth our effort to dig them out of the beanbags to let them weave a trolling spread into monofilament twine.

We picked up a spunky Bonita on the troll and one good gag grouper. I had to prod to get them to deal with the details of reeling in each of the two fish. The rolling trolling was on-the-clock time well spent.

After catching a few more quality live baits by hook and line, I rolled on to a tree-line, visible waypoint I named "Train Wreck." This spot will either hot rock your world or sit you on a block of ice. It is weird how some spots can be that way. If you're in the neighborhood, you just got to try it, because you never know how it is going to turnout. This time....

After getting the second line out, the first rod bowed down hard! "Fish on," I announced loudly, just to be a mean reminder of the night before. However, by this time, the hangover part was waning. The hang-on part was on. Jake coached the sobered angler on how to bring in the fish. The battle was a bizarre mix that mimicked the digging battle of a grouper coupled with the run-off spurts of a cobia. In time, the fish showed color. It was an offshore breeder-bull redfish. A shoal of new-penny copper escorted all around that fish at the surface. It was one of those moments I wish could be witnessed by more anglers. Magnificent to see, a brilliant sheet of moving copper!

From that point on, it was bent over rod and bent over rod, regardless of what bait was tossed. "Don't put another bait out. We're too busy releasing to handle any more." Our fishing was locked down to the two original rods out of excessive activity. The bull red fish were waist long on a tall man. This type of action would be hype on TV. The "Train Wreck" happened though without the typical actors of grouper and/or cobia on board.

Eventually, the herd of big red fish swam through. Thankfully. The ride in was a wet glass slide with the sun-ball dipping into the sea off the starboard stern. The setting sun was as red as their eyes earlier in the morning. Now, I was seeing red because of the botched forecast.

The seas are the heart's blood of the earth.
Henry Beston

Turtle Hunting

It was early September, and it was going to be a hot one, according to the forecast. Typical Florida summer marine weather, sea breeze in the morning until the land and sea temps equilibrate, the heat index will climb to uncomfortable, seas will get ice rink slick, and anvil headed thunder storms will develop over land to threaten the ride home.

Slick waters are great for traveling across but not necessarily great for fishing. Perhaps the lack of energy in the water puts the fish on holiday, free to roam, unhindered by the rush of current. I don't know exactly why; maybe someone else understands it, but history has proven to me, slick waters are difficult to catch fish in.

We did a quick stop to fish up some live bait off the flats. A nice load of pinfish, pigfish, spot-tail pinfish, and porgies came quickly and was a fun activity. On the ride out, I engaged in light conversation and answered the FAQs. The motors sounded smooth in synchronicity. They were recently serviced at Paul's Boat Repair in Jena, and the girls purred in appreciation of good touch. It wasn't long before the stereo purr, combined with the casual roll of my boat, *CAT NAP*, lulled folks into a deep daydream of what might come that day.

I was left to think about what to do during the forthcoming slick water. The previous night, the land temperature remained hot, low eighties. Sea temperature was eighty-eight degrees Fahrenheit. The differential between land and sea temperature was slight, meaning the sea breeze would not be sustained long enough to make wave action. Furthermore, I was moving quickly offshore, out of the influence of the sea breeze, so I expected to war against the influence of a slick sea all day. On the happy side, anchoring wouldn't be necessary.

The simple strategy was to acknowledge the liberty of not needing the anchor and plan on hitting more spots in the same time to make-up for the expected lack of bite—in addition, more than welcome the machinegun peck bite of Florida snapper to fill in the lulls. To "Welcome" the Florida snapper meant scaling down the hook and bait sizes. The Florida snapper is the chicken of our Gulf, greatly enjoyed by all, yet it gets no respect. It should be renamed "Rodney Dangerfield" since no one brags on catching them, yet so many fill their coolers with them and smile doing so.

Anyway, I was relying on the Dangerfield snapper bite, the ease of movement without the anchor, and a touch of sleight-of-hand on my part to bring in a good day of fishing. Two hours after our first baits went down, it was going fair, better than expected, or, best said, "It was what it was." It was slow. Even the Ravenous Rodney's weren't constant ratta-tat-tatting the baits, just an occasional short salvo, enough to keep an angler's attention.

What to do? I couldn't go along like this all day, I'd go crazy even if we ended up with a good box of fish. Fishing, to me, is far more than dumping a chunk of bait on the sea floor and waiting to see if some fish takes it before a crab cleans it off, or I have to bring it up to throw it away.

Thinking, while looking out on the horizon, I saw the lump of a loggerhead turtle on the surface fifty yards from the boat. I watched it a few minutes before it raised its helmeted head to look around and grab a breath. It was a cool scene I usually pointed out and shared with folks, but at the time I didn't want the awareness to break my thoughts. Yet, I looked left and right and then around to find there were many turtle lumps, some with heads up, all around the boat, close and far away.

Turtles frequently come up for air over the good bottom they reside on. I thought how awesome it was to see so many turtles and I pointed them out to those focused down their line. It was cool! Everybody started talking. There was a big one. There was a huge one. There was a baby one. There were two. Talk went on and on; it broke the boredom. It broke the monotony of my mind because I saw the sign pop up in a featureless sea.

I decided to use the turtle happening to our, well, my advantage. It required that I give a quick simple "Why we're changing things and doing this like this now," discourse.

The briefing filled in why, what, and how for the crew. It gave our collective movements purpose. It made the crew tighten up. It excited all for the expectation of catching fish. It excited me about being led to new bottom.

And it worked! No, not one turtle spot loaded the boat, but some fish were caught at each. Most of the fish were nothing to brag about, but some pasted a memory on someone's Facebook. Basically, it gave us a pleasurable purpose we could see and pursue.

It ended up being a great, fun-filled day just hunting floating turtles, and exploring what lay beneath them. Sometimes one has to look out and see the sign to change the course of the day.

All veteran anglers have their tricks of the trade...usually you have to fish a long time to pick them up.
Wheeler Johnson

Joel and the Fish

Joel pitched out a small Whoop Ass jig, searching for a tussle with a Spanish mackerel. The rest of us watched the live bait rods, hoping for a run-in with a cobia, king, or whatever, large enough to make us yell, "Live action." Spanish mackerel were darting around in the swarms of small bait around the boat, so fishing for them was a reasonable way to pass time.

"Got one," yelled Joel. Some of us turned to show some support; others just kept watching the rods for the big bend over. This wasn't the first Spanish hook-up of the morning. He was fishing a spinning combo commonly used for trout, loaded with ten-pound test. The light gear meant that the squeal of the drag was to be expected. But after a few minutes of tussle, the battle wasn't coming to a close. We figured this out when the drag squealed off a prolonged blast.

What in this world have you got? I thought. A king had taken the Spanish, he supposedly had, and was taking off to the other side of the Gulf. His line was headed off towards the bow, shrieking the reel drag so high pitched one of the guys howled. Our mate, Jake, helped Joel over and through the beanbags onto the bow as the fish went from starboard to port. Joel dropped down from the port bow and got some line collected back. The fish swung back towards the stern. Joel stepped along following the fish. The guys fishing off the port rolled in their gear and let him pass through. Soon enough, the guys on starboard needed to roll up their gear to let Joel pass through on his way, again, to the bow. By then, we had flopped both beanbags in front of the console to allow Joel free looping.

Up on the bow a second time went Joel. One of his buddies was holding him steady by gripping his belt. He had gathered up enough

94

line so that when the fish swung hard to port, it cruised underneath the anchor rode. Jake did a belly flop, was handed the rod, passed it underneath the anchor, rode, and gave it back to Joel to continue on. Down the portside gunnel came Joel. Again the guys who had recast their baits had to reel in to let Joel pass.

The fish took a long strut off the stern to Joel's chagrin. "Every time I get him close, he takes off," Joel, groused.

It was true. Each time he seemed to be gaining line, the fish charged off twice as much, sometimes to the point the spool became woefully skinny.

The reel he was using had a large capacity for ten-pound test mono, so getting skinny meant the fish was at a distant latitude/longitude away from Joel. The line on the spool was fairly fresh, yet not yesterday fresh.

The spin combo was a Walmart special I had bought a dozen of, basically, for trout and bait fishing. The maintenance routine for that collection of combos was a daily rinse of fresh water and an occasional squirt of WD-40. The gear was considered annually disposable.

The others had good anticipation Joel was going to land the fish. I hoped he could land the fish as well, but my expectations were burdened, knowing the history of the equipment. I didn't bother to tell anyone that information.

Joel went around the boat track four more times and twice again passed under the anchor rode before the guys attempting to fish from the cockpit finally hung their rods on the T-top or rocket launcher due to frustration and respect. They decided instead of fishing, to form a cheerleading squad by snacking, drinking beer, and coach yelling the good and bad. Joel was our entertainment who was becoming weary of the same old act.

My thought of a kingfish engulfing a Spanish mackerel, by now, had changed to a bull redfish encounter. Previously, in another part of the Gulf at the same approximate depth, we had stumbled upon a mass school of bull reds. They bulldozed everything we tossed to them until we quit each other.

I was sure Joel had a bull red. It was a signature fight of tug and run. I was most confident when I saw a squaretail on the surface, well away in the glare of the sun.

Five more times Joel went around the track. The guys hollered as he was pulled to each corner of the boat, like NASCAR fans on the turns. Once he was asked if he wanted to hand off the rod. His answer back was such that the question was never asked again.

Though I thought it would never end this way, the fish was tiring, and being brought closer and closer to the boat. The ten-pound Trilene Big Game was giving an anonymous testimony to all but me. Toward the end of the battle, the fish swam by just under the surface. It was an unexpected, large amberjack.

Jake stalked the fish to and fro along the gunnel behind Joel like a lioness waiting for the best opportunity to make the kill. Jake felt the pressure of the hour and fifteen minute pursuit. Jake was in charge of the kill. In an instant, all could be for naught! The spring of the gaff shot had to be on target. There was no second chance, considering the ten-pound test and the wear and tear it had endured. The line was spent. The fish was spent. And…, Joel was spent. It was a one shot deal for Jake.

The thud of a twenty some pound amberjack sounded on the deck, followed by yips, hollers, yells, and high fives, fist bumps, hugs, and other actions that stay on my floating Vegas named *Cat Nap*. Joel was *Rocky* on saltwater. He fought the fight well and beat his Apollo.

The rest of the day went fine but nothing happened that usurped what Joel accomplished in the first half of the day. Cheers to Joel.

It's not the size of the dog in the fight but the size of the fight in the dog.
Mark Twain

JAWS

Enclosure

The Delta Airline crew from 'Hotlanta': Steve, Chris, Darrell, Mike, Steven, and Terry flew into town Tuesday evening, locked and loaded for a one-day offshore trip and a second day inshore fishing excursion. At least that was the plan on the books.

The first day offshore was a grand success. The weather was perfect. The fish were cooperative, but most importantly, these guys were just plain fun. We had a ball, as if we had been lifetime friends. It was a frat party with a fishing theme.

We started the morning with a forty-five minute bait-catching jam. My bait traps had been recently "forever borrowed," so we had to use hook and line to catch our live bait for the day. Porgies, pinfish, spot-tail pinfish, squirrelfish, and some large grunts came over the gunnel at a good clip.

"This is like bream fishing," Chris announced.

"If we don't do anything but this all day, I'll be happy," said Mike.

Steve looked strangely at a large grunt and said, "Bait captain?"

I smiled and said "Yea, don't be scared." We all laughed.

In short order, we were off to a hard bottom with ledges for grouper fishing.

The first two drops produced a few grouper too short to harvest. Trolling between stops put a couple keeper grouper in the box. The third drop, a two foot ledge, paid in spades. The grouper were there, and the bite was in the ""on position."

"Oh my God, the porgy never made the bottom," Darrel hollered. That hot grouper bite caused a spontaneous hallelujah eruption from a newly planted floating congregation of primitive, southern, non-denominational, Pentecostal sinners, like me, rejoicing aboard the

"First Church of the Gulf of Mexico," thirty-two-foot, Twin Vee catamaran boat I originally named Cat Nap.

I was near Terry when he blurted, "Jesus Christ."

"I believe Jesus is going to let you work through this tribulation on your own, my brother," I said in passing.

I love to hear folk praise the Lord. I'm a Christian myself and enjoy testimony even from those convicted under the spirited pressure of a bent-double fishing pole. I hope they may mean what they're saying, at least for the moment, recognizing the need for help from above, or at least above waterline.

A large grouper was pulling Terry's broomstick rod down and line from a 'locked down' drag was digging its way to rocky reef below.

"Reel man, reel!" I yelled and coached.

"It won't reel," Terry groaned.

"Pull up; reel down," I encouraged.

With help from above, he got the gist of the grouper sermon and brought the fish to the boat.

The other guys, even the one or two sleeping through the grouper sermon, caught fish. In an hour or so, the fish box had a fine offering. The sleepy guys had to have the offering plate—bait bucket—passed by them more often with bait before they finally got the message and chipped in to help full the coffer fish box.

A submerged wreck was five miles away. In fifteen minutes we were met with fifteen to thirty-pound amberjacks guarding the ill-fated tug. Steve, Chris, and Darrell started flipping two ounce, white, buck-tailed jigs on large spinning outfits. Instantly, "string music" played from the reels. On the other side, Mike, Steven, and Terry free lined livies. At any given time, one or more of the men were bent over singing praises. The "First Church of the Gulf of Mexico" had a choir with an orchestra. Amberjacks swarmed the boat to the delight of the airline employees.

"Captain, we should have just come here in the first place," Mike said.

"I like to mix it up a bit," I replied.

We limited on jacks within twenty minutes, but the crew played catch and release for two hours until all but one had had enough.

Darrell, the youngest and smallest of the bunch—better said scrawny—noticed the fighting belts strapped on either side of the T-top soon after boarding. He announced, "I want to catch a fish big enough so I'll need one of those!"

I mentioned jewfish, renamed Goliath grouper for political correctness. I told him jewfish can grow to one thousand pounds. The average manageable size caught is between two hundred and two hundred fifty pounds. I also mentioned jewfish are federally protected; thus we're not allowed to fish for them, but it was possible to catch one accidentally.

Darrell became obsessed with the chance to tug on a fish of that size and power. I told him I'd let him know when the opportunity was available. He asked about it everywhere we stopped.

"It's time Darrell!" I wished his name were David just for the irony of him going up against Goliath, but alas.

Darrell strapped on a fighting belt and stood proud as if it had the word "CHAMPION" written on the front. His buddies took one look at him and unloaded commentary. "At least I got the stones to do it!"

"Speaking of which, always put the butt of the rod in the cup of the fighting belt, never between your legs," I suggested.

After we limited on amberjack, one amberjack was gut hooked and died while playing catch and release. I cross cut that fish in thirds for bait. From the rocket launcher behind the captain's bench, I pulled a rod and reel combo and said for all to hear, "This is the Super Man pole."

Darrell took it from my hand and put it in the cup of the fighting belt like he was carrying a flag in a parade.

"Yea boys, Super Man pole."

After his gyrations, you didn't want to salute it.

The Super Man pole consisted of a 9/0 Penn reel with a hammered down drag attached to a stubby five-foot tuna stick loaded with one-hundred-pound, test monofilament. It was pre-rigged with a three-foot section of two hundred pound test mono leader connected to the mainline via a loop-to-loop knot. A 14/0 hook was tied to the end of the leader. I used a small piece of string to fasten a ten ounce sinker where the mainline and leader joined. I hooked the head section on the meat hook.

"Are you ready?"

"Born ready!!!"

"Pull up a foot, then reel down a foot and repeat. Never let your hand get pinned between the rod and the gunnel." I reiterated. "And never put the butt of the rod between your legs!"

Then, as Darrell stood there, holding what looked like a tire rim welded to a piece of rebar with parachute cord dangling a Smithfield ham, he asked the crazy question: "How will I know when I get a bite?"

Somehow I managed an answer in an analogy. "Do you remember when you were a boy waiting on the corner for the school bus? When it came along, it stopped, the door opened up, and you went inside. Then the bus drove away. Think of yourself as the bait."

He lowered the bait down to the corner. The bus came within minutes. The bus swam away, pulling the rod over.

"Well, stop the bus; reel it up," I said.

"It won't…Oh God…reel," lamented Darrell.

A few yards of line groaned off the locked down drag then stopped. Darrell yelled crazy again, "I got you now!" He started to pull up and reel down. He did that twice, then more line peeled off the reel and stopped. I was standing behind him, holding on to the belt.

"Now I got you!" said Darrell. He got three pumps in, and then more line came off the reel.

Before he could say anything more, I said, "The bus is just picking up more kids."

Everyone but Darrell busted up, and the bus took off for a long ride to school. POW! Line broke.

Darrell had the look of a redneck after saying, "Hey ya'll watch this!" Who would have thought it could have turned out so wrong?

All the warning signs were in place. The fighting belt that looked like it was in the battle, not the prize of a battle. The medieval looking gear said to be used for fishing. The fishing line was stout enough a hangman could use it. A hook so big a blacksmith could forge it. The bait large enough to be served on a platter to a family at Thanksgiving. Then the analogy of a bus used as the example of a fish named Goliath. And last, but certainly not least, none of your friends were willing to participate with you.

"Set it up Captain. I want to try it again."

I turned to Darrell and asked, "Are you high?" I turned to his buddies and asked, "Is he off his meds?"

Steven piped up, "He's just crazy."

"A fact we already established," I said.

It took a few minutes of re-rigging before I hooked the eight-pound mid-section for bait. "Darrell, these hooks cost me two dollars and fifty cents each," I said in play.

100

He reached in his jeans pocket, pulled out a ten-dollar bill, slapped it on the captain's bench, and said, "I'm in for three more hooks then."

I had to ask a rhetorical question, "Did you ride the short bus to school?"

Darrell was back in action. Again, the pole slowly bent over. Again, Darrell tried to turn the fish. Again, the line broke; strike two.

"I still got two more hooks coming, Captain."

Re-rigged and baited with the tail section, we watched Darrell as if he were the black guy in an old horror movie, trying not to become too emotionally attached, because we knew the brother wasn't going to make it to the end. Bang! The fish hit.

"Arrrrrgh!" Again, Darrell felt the strain of a huge fish.

Amazingly, the line began to peel off the reel as though I hadn't locked the drag down with pliers. Luckily, the fish moved away from the wreck, and then two men quickly hand pulled the anchor. I loosened the reel drag a touch. We started a crazy journey across the Gulf.

Darrell held the fish, the fish towed the boat, and the rest of us were there for the ride. He asked for water. One of the guys cracked a bottle of water open and held it to Darrell's mouth.

"No, I don't want to drink it; just pour it on my head."

The older guys laughed while baptizing him. It was hot as Hades. Darrell did like his water chilled but fermented as well.

After twenty long minutes, the previously UFO—unknown fish object—appeared below. Jewfish? No, shark. A seven-foot sand shark had taken the bait, and somehow, he hadn't cut the mono leader. When it noticed the boat, it discontinued the slow tow approach and began to thrash more wildly. In time, that change in behavior allowed a tooth to touch the line, cutting it like a razor.

The release of tension threw Darrell back on his butt for a not so glorious ending. He was bumped, yet still pumped. His left forearm looked Popeye style. The veins were some sort of inter-city roadway map under tight skin.

It was time to return to port, but I posed an opportunity to the crew before heading back. "Tomorrow we could trout fish as planned, or if ya'll give me the first half of the day to scout for new grouper numbers, the rest of the day, ya'll could play with the amberjack and such. Think about it on the ride." They chose the offshore option right off the bat.

The next day after bait collection, we headed out thirty-five miles

101

and began trolling, scouting for new bottom for me. The two aft trolling rods were stiff each set up with a #6 commercial stainless steel diving planer. A planer is a trolling device attached to the end of the main line that forces bait or lure to be presented deeper in the water column than they would normally go without the aid of the planner. Tethered to the end of each planner using a twenty foot leader were two Rapala CD 18s. On the two forward trolling rods were Mann's Stretch 30 deep diving lures tied straight on. It was a simple trolling spread that allowed us to place the lures near the bottom to target grouper.

It was the ultimate day for scouting new bottom; the sea was slick calm. However, it is always most difficult to get a grouper to bite when the sea has no energy. It seems the fish become as lazy as the water. Lizardfish, smaller than the lures themselves, hit the plugs a couple of times. That broke the boredom, but essentially, it just fouled the trolling set-up, no grouper.

The crew saw a slumbering turtle ahead and brought it to my attention. I was locked-eyed on to the sonar display and would have missed it. I trolled toward it. Turtles are natural indicators of quality habitat. It is where they grocery shop. They're not necessarily long-term residents on any one spot, but they certainly spend time in the fish department.

We came within twenty feet before he awoke and scooted to the bottom. The bottom below him was alive. I decided to stop trolling and drop some baits down. I put the engines in neutral.

"Let's bring in the trolling rods."

"Captain, what's that?" The tip of a fin was barely above the waterline ahead of the boat.

"Small shark," I said, not paying it much attention. I've seen so many sharks. I was busy watching the four guys bring the lines in and ready to coach away preventable line tangles. Our mate, Little John, was doing the same thing. The deep trolling gear has much resistance through the water, making slow work to bring it back to the boat; the reel in takes time and coordination.

While they were reeling in the trolling gear, the fin casually came to investigate us. The two men not working the four rods watched its leisurely meander toward us. Finally, the fin made it to us and cruised the boat. The two were shocked at what they saw and squawked, "Ya'll gotta see this!"

The fin was attached to a ten-foot, female mako shark with a five-foot, enamored jake in tow below her.

Ten foot wasn't an exaggerated guess. I measured it as it swam abroad the twelve-foot beam of the boat. It was a beautiful animal demanding respect. It got all of our respect when it rose from the water and laid its head on the dive platform between the outboard motors, spaced ten foot apart, swinging back and forth to check us out. The pucker factor lasted mere seconds before she slipped back in the water, but the memory will go in the ground with me…and more than likely with the rest of the guys as well.

Bad timing. When the shark slipped back into the water, the two abandoned stern rods equipped with the planers outfits were close behind the boat—too close. We all cautiously walked back to the stern to watch the big mako inhale of two Rapala CD 18s and one #6 planer. There was no fight. The lines were cut instantly. Forty-five dollars' worth of equipment swallowed. I was still caught up in the moment.

The shark remained with the boat long enough to allow my buddy, Little John, to remove a Stretch 30 lure from a wire leader trolling combo and replace it with an 8/0 hook and pin on a dead lizardfish we'd caught previously. He let the lizardfish sink down with a handful of sardines as chum.

I noticed, saying, "John, that's just #5 wire for kingfish."

"It is the best we got for the now," he snapped. He had a point, but the tackle was weak, too weak to handle the job.

Amazingly, after sucking in a large chunk of stainless steel, two long wooden sticks with heavy double treble hooks attached, and the stiff line that strung all that together in its gullet, the shark still had an appetite. The shark moved through the sinking fish, taking a couple sardines. Then it took the lizardfish. John set the hook and handed the pole to Steve as line rolled off the reel. Apparently, the hook was set away from the rows of teeth.

The shark sounded on the starboard side and raced under the boat to port stutter, stepping Steve around with the rod tip forced below the water line. A WOW atmosphere enveloped the boat. It was just starting.

In two minutes, the first unexpected Kodak moment occurred. The shark launched straight up, tail ten feet above the water. It splashed down like a cow falling from the sky. Guys were scrabbling for cameras.

I was dumbfounded, seeing a three-hundred-pound, wild fish blow

103

from the water like a missile. How did the hook stick? Why didn't the line part? It was happening again! Click, click, digital Kodak time. It was beautiful to watch...a once in a lifetime moment. Then I had an awful thought, *"What if that shark jumped in the boat?"*

And right then Darrell came up beside me and asked the crazy, "Captain, how we going to get that fish in the boat?"

I didn't have to answer. The shark soared a third time and rolled over the line, breaking it. There was no real disappointment. The experience was the prize.

I knew it was coming but not in unison, the line straight from the movie *Jaws.* "Captain, you need a bigger boat."

Lord, suffer me to catch a fish so large that even I in talking of it
afterward shall have no need to lie.
Motto: Herbert Hoover's Fishing Lodge

Me Lucky Charm

We had been underway for around twenty minutes.

"Daddy, when we going to fish?" Seth asked his dad, Kip.

"Son, I don't know" Kip answered.

I had to over hear them because Seth was sitting to my right on the captain's bench, and Kip was standing to my left. They were speaking across me.

"All water is not created equal; we have to ride to where the fish are. You should have read that in the e-mail I sent you. First a boat ride; then we fish," I said as animated as a Shakespearean actor on stage, complete with arm movements punctuated with a stern face at the end.

Seth looked at me saying nothing verbally, but his face clearly stated, "You're nuts, and you didn't answer my question Mr. Boat-Driver."

"Fifteen minutes longer," I said in my normal voice.

He took the extra fifteen minutes as if I told him he was going to miss summer vacation before we started fishing. Thirty minutes of not doing what you really want to do is a very, very, very long time for a boy.

Honesty naturally oozes out of most children. It can be conveyed verbally, by expression or action, but can't be hidden. They don't know why to hide it. They live, by and large, in the right now of life. The future seems too long to wait for, even when cruising along on a nice boat for five more minutes. That isn't acceptable torture to endure. Seth was dealing in this moment of his life, and obviously, the boat was moving along too slowly to keep up with his tempo.

Seth was seven and a half, "going on eight." He didn't just like fishing; he loved it. His dad told me Seth fished every day in a pond in their neighborhood. He had his own fishing pole and tackle box. I realized I was sitting next to myself forty some years ago. To take his mind off the time, I asked him about school, what kind of work he did, and if he was married. That tactic absorbed ten minutes.

Sea conditions were sloppy to rough. We would need to jump back and fish the grass flats if things got worse, but for the moment, it was safe but slow going. We made our way to a small rock outcrop that should hold some sheepshead. I made an educated guess, and the anchor was tossed. At anchor, we were bow dipping, taking a little water over the front. The wind and tide were both strong, somewhat conflicting. The forces at odds made anchoring difficult. The anchor never grabbed solid, always inching backward. It was impossible to stay put even with playing out more scope on the rode. However, when the boat swung near the rocks, Seth picked up a sheepshead.

"Got one!" I heard.

I turned to see him reeling up a sheepy. Someone would be there with a net and dip the fish aboard. Seth, and nobody else, managed to pick up three fish and a juvenile gag grouper. Charles, the mate, was working the boat with me. He had just loaded the anchor back aboard after it gave away. He didn't mind wrestling that anchor umpteen times, but he needed some relief, re-anchoring is frustrating work. We needed to do something different.

Charles said, "It seems to be laying down a bit."

I looked around and saw it was abating. The air temperature was warming up and backing down the shore breeze. The wind was blowing in the direction—meaning a comfortable ride—of an area of hard bottom that was covered with ravenous Florida snapper known as white grunt. That would be a *super* Seth fish ticket. I planned to run with it for twenty minutes or so and then troll a couple of plugs back for another twenty minutes. The time trolling would span a period to insure conditions were indeed improving. I equate weather to a woman, lovingly unpredictable, best to allow time to see how she is going to swing before proceeding. Simple advice from a captain who has been "tossed in the salt" due to a stupid assumption at sea, as well as, from experience gleaned by my lovely ever-changing wife of twenty-five years on land. It is always best to proceed with closed mouth caution.

The overall goal was to bring Seth to a Florida snapper feeding festival where the action would be speedy and *super*. Seth would have the time of his life. I knew a forty-minute boat ride was asking a lot, but I hoped that catching a fish while trolling might shrink time in his mind.

Time was the issue in more ways to me than Seth. It doesn't take much time for the Gulf to smooth out. Conversely, it doesn't take long to get raw. But again, time is still measured differently in the mind of a boy. There is now, and forever from now.

Seth asked his dad, "Daddy, when are we going to fish?"

I intervened, "We're venturing forth to a spot in the Gulf where the fish are plentiful. I found it while plundering about; arrrgh Matey," I said pirate style. "We'll start in fifteen minutes."

He looked at me as if I'd said, "Life plus ten years."

"How do you know fifteen minutes, Capt. B?" Seth asked. I pointed out the GPS on the bottom left where that information was displayed. From that moment on, Seth was armed with information. There was no tricking the boy from then on.

"How much longer Seth?" I'd ask.

"Seven minutes" he said.

"Thank you, Navigator," I responded.

"The machine says zero, and we're still going," Seth brought to my attention.

"Well, during the last minute of the journey the machine gets a little confused; it goes haywire. I don't know why we need the confounded thing in the first place. Let's turn it off," I spouted in hidden jest.

"No, I like looking at it," Seth told me.

"OK, if you say so, Navigator," I uttered, sounding like the salty sea captain.

"That other machine is sonar; it lets me view the bottom," I told Seth. It displayed in color, and he liked that. I called it my fish TV.

"What's that other thing?" he asked.

"That is the radio in case I have to call the fish," I lied.

I slowed the boat down to trolling speed and winked at Charles. Unnoticed to Seth, Charles and Kip quietly set back two trolling plugs. We were twenty minutes from where I wanted to "party with the Florida snapper." In the back of my mind, I was hoping a grouper or two would ambush the offerings just to break up our journey.

"Daddy, why aren't we fishing?" Seth asked.

Kip said, "We are fishing."

I jumped into the conversation, trying to explain the art of grouper trolling, or trolling in general, but that facet of fishing hadn't been upgraded into Seth's fishing program. For Seth, trolling was a synonym for boat riding. It took the entire twenty minute drag before a sparkle of lime rock with live growth on it showed up on the *Nickelodeon* sonar screen, and seconds later both poles bent over. Oh happy day! I wished it had happened many questions ago, but I was glad it happened at all.

One grouper passed the bar, and the other was tossed back. I made a couple more passes over my new waypoint I named "Seth1," picking up some more fish, though small and non-keepers. It was still needed action.

The sea had calmed down well by then. Seth was in prime mode to drop bait to whatever would eat it. I was ready to play fish toss myself. The trolling rods were put away, and we cruised ahead for ten minutes to a big area of lime rock bottom that crawled with Florida snapper. Anchoring didn't have to be perfect; the area was large.

Just like I wanted, every piece of shrimp put down on Seth's hook resulted in a dandy Florida snapper or a hump-head sea bass. Kip eventually took up a snapper pole and joined in the fun, adding fish to the box. I became Seth's personal fishing assistant. While I was de-hooking fish, tossing them in the cooler, and re-baiting, Seth and I became good buddies.

Charles was off on the other side, chicken-rigging with a jig and an extra hook, popping doubles. Seth was easing into hambone class, reeling up fish after fish. The fish box was filling up quickly with hump head sea bass and Florida snapper pushing two pounds or better. Seth declared shrimp the ultimate Florida snapper bait—until we ran out of shrimp and I substituted squid strips. Seth had doubts; however, the squid worked just as well and had durability to last longer on the hook.

Then Seth, self-declared professional angler, told the rest of us he could catch fish on anything, which leads back to the title of this story. Seth's mom had packed him and his dad a big goody bag for a lunch: caramel popcorn with peanuts, candies, sandwiches, drinks of various flavors, other surprises, and Lucky Charms mini-marshmallows the colors of a psychedelic rainbow. We had been popping mini-marshmallows in our mouths. The opened bag was on the captain's bench.

"Captain, why don't we use marshmallows?" Seth asked.

At that moment, the fish box was well padded, and I was floating around on Seth's euphoric cloud.

"Why not," I answered.

I shook a small handful of puffs into my hand and pinned one marshmallow on his hook, and we sent it to the bottom. The outcome was unknown for three seconds!

"Got one!" Seth declared.

His pole doubled over, and quickly Seth rolled a big Florida snapper splashing to the surface. I unhooked it and tossed it in the box. I hooked on another marshmallow, and Seth sent it down. Was the first fish a fluke? In the fish frenzy below, did this fish take whatever was available? Apparently not, for fish after fish made passage into the fish box through the new magic of rainbow colored marshmallows. Marshmallows are a lot cheaper than shrimp or squid and never rot. I found out we, as well as the Florida snapper, enjoy the sweet treat from a boy.

You can never stop learning. Think about it. I would have never realized marshmallows were Florida snapper bait. It took a child who knew no different and whimsically baited outside the lines of fishing to teach me something new. The episode caused me to do some after fishing thinking.

I'm a professional charter captain, experienced with over four decades of fishing. I've read countless books, magazines and newspaper articles about fishing, sorted through a load of more stories/lies than I can recall. I'm confident I don't know everything about fishing, but I'm well versed in a multitude of techniques to catch a vast variety of fish, fresh and salt. Yet in one simple moment, I listened to a boy with nothing to lose and learned something new.

That is why fishing is great. It is forever dynamic. The thrill is in the journey. Boys and girls of all ages enjoy it. The time to go fishing is at your call. It can be taken as serious as you choose or as loose as a soft marshmallow on the end of a hook. Take a kid and a bag of marshmallows fishing next time with a thermos of hot chocolate as back up. The game looms; make time to enjoy.

A man should never stop learning, even on his last day.
Maimondes

Touch of Seasoned Women

Recently, I've had charters that fortunately involved women. Most of the women came with their husbands, yet two trips were women only! You can imagine the vast majority of my trips are men only. Now, I'm not about to throw-down on men, because I happen to be one myself. However....

Women bring something extra to the game, as well as a lot more stuff to the boat. A lot of that stuff is delicious by the way.

If asked, "Would you like to try some homemade...? Homemade is the operative word. My answer is an enthusiastic, "Yes," usually, before they have time to finish the question. And I have no idea what I've volunteered to eat but know full well it's going to be fantastic. And it is scrumptious, and I rave, and they smile, and all is good.

The women I've taken fishing lately have been seasoned. That doesn't necessarily mean in terms of fishing. For a couple of gals, it was their first time fishing. It was literally, "This thingy is called a fishing reel, and it is attached to a stick called a fishing pole. Do this and the fishing *string* will come off the reel. When the string, most often called line, stops going off the reel, the bait, you called fish food, is on the bottom. Wind the line taut, so you can feel the heavy thing called a sinker. When you feel something unusual, that being telegraph tapping, heaviness, or a yank down, yank up, and start reeling in the line."

"Oh, and while you're winding in the string, through the stick with hoops, onto the thingy, stick your left foot out, and shake it all about," I say in humor. That keeps the atmosphere loose and fun.

I'm not going to let a first-timer feel they are goofing-up and ruining the trip for all. It's just a stupid fish after all.

Most of the ladies had limited experience. They told me about head boats, trips on a friend's boat, and/or with their hubbies on "the family" boat. On a head boat, you're a tourist. On a friend's boat, you're a guest, and unless you're an avid fisherwoman, a very desirable yet oh so rare breed, the boat he bought for "us" is really for him. The family occasions are compromises to keep everyone else happy so he can have the boat.

On the high financial flip side, a side I've rarely been a guest on, he may have bought a yacht to wrap a woman in some very luxurious and expensive fiberglass. The amenities consist of what you'd expect at a five star-hotel, including staff. It's a win-win but costs big-big. However, if you can afford all that, it would still be better to charter a boat anywhere on earth than own one yacht at one place. If you're thinking, "We could trailer it." Stop. Yachts don't have trailers. Besides, it would require a locomotive with tires as the tow vehicle, and the yacht wouldn't pass under any overpass.

One lady, Virginia, nicknamed Ginny—in her seventies—may have had more float-time than me. She had tales, from wade fishing for bream and bass in Okeechobee amongst the reptiles, to offshore fishing out of you-name-a-place on earth. I hung on each storyline like a fish.

My first outing with Ginny and best friends Regina and Linda was a half-day sheepshead trip, because it was rough in the morning but supposed to lay down in the afternoon. Ginny sat beside me on the captain's bench. When we passed Lazy Island into the open Gulf, I could see a two-to-three-foot hard chop.

The Gulf is a strange body of water in that the waves can have no direction and no backsides. The seas don't have to be big to be gnarly. It was just a six-mile trip, but within two miles, we had to stop and apply raingear. While they were suiting up, I said, "This ain't no kidnapping. Whenever you've had enough, we'll head in."

Ginny said, "Put us on the fish."

I slow boated to the spot. However, by the time we got there, Regina was in the grip of the dancing, twirling Sea Monkey. I understood why she was seasick because I had to double anchor to keep the boat from sliding backwards. Then Ginny told me she and Linda had poor balance. I thought about how much I didn't need to be out here. Nevertheless, Regina sat on the captain's bench with a great attitude. Ginny sat on a cooler with a handful of frozen shrimp beside her, fishing pole in hand, and was already started. Linda sat in the rear seat as I gave the how-to to the first timer. She wasn't quick to pick up how the reel worked. However, in the laughter, Linda brought in the

111

first sheepshead. Ginny was a duck on water. I kept the shrimp coming, and she kept bringing in the fish. I even caught a couple between dipping fish for the ladies. It worked out better than I thought. And, yes, we were all happy when Ginny said, "Captain, we're ready."

What did the women have in common? They were all cool, daring, courageous, brave women who brought with them a boatload of happiness, encouragement, and hopefulness, even when things didn't turn out just as planned. One thing I've noticed about women: if one has trouble reeling in a fish or with anything else, the others come in to help and give encouragement. On the other hand, a man with troubles is an island subject to ridicule from his friends.

Did the ladies catch fish? Every time. Honestly, it is not unusual for the women to out-fish the men. They have a secret called touch.

Next to God, we are indebted to women, first for life itself,
and then for making it worth having.
C. Nesteil Bovee

A Change of Pace

It was mid-day, mid-August under a sky that had a few motionless, cotton-ball clouds. The Gulf of Mexico was oily slick. A high-pressure system had been under control for several days. I was portside, mid-ship with rod in hand, trying to feel a fish bite that would not happen. Though tucked under whatever shade was available to me, sweat was pouring off me from head to toe. I looked down at my legs, and rivulets of water were running from my knees over my calves and into my Crocs. It seemed I had an internal sprinkler system discharging full blast. The oppressive heat was like being pressed under an atmospheric waffle iron. It was wicked hot!

All but one of my anglers was done enjoying fishing. They were also done in terms of being slow cooked for hours over a Gulf of hot saltwater and a stellar heater that kept getting hotter as the day progressed.

I had been sucking down water since the motors popped off that morning, three quarts, but yet to go pee. Not a good sign. I was losing more fluid than I was taking in. Honestly, I'm a profuse sweater, so I need to rehydrate more than some folks. I watched folks on the boat, encouraged them to drink water—not cold beer—and try to see if they urinate—an indication of hydration.

***

Ladies, using the restroom is as natural as breathing. It is poor judgment to deny healthy hydration to avoid the embarrassment of using the head. So *drink up*! Gentlemen understand even if the only course of action is the five-gallon boat bucket. Anyway…for males or females, heat exhaustion is a serious first step to heat stroke. It is as simple as drinking water to avoid a severe medical situation.

***

I had one dehydration situation result in a life-flight. It scared everyone, even those on the other side of the radio. The EMTs, who boarded us while en route, were some brave, well-trained, and prepared individuals who should get paid more than they do. We were welcomed back with an ambulance crew that took him to the waiting helicopter. He took a twenty-thousand-dollar flight due to the lack of water! Water costs less than a dollar a gallon.

Other than drinking water, more cool tricks are getting in whatever shade available, wetting down your head and the rest of your body with a soaking wet towel—freshwater is best, but saltwater is OK. Draping a sopping wet towel around your neck feels great, as does misting yourself using a squirt bottle filled with a half and half mix of water and rubbing alcohol. It can be fun to mist yourself and friends regularly. The evaporative cooling of alcohol feels wonderful and is revitalizing!

The "dog days" of summer are the toughest times to catch fish. When you're hot, do you feel like eating? Neither do the fish bathing in water ninety degrees plus. If water isn't moving across to cool them like a ceiling fan over your bed, they go inactive.

Experienced fishermen know to best catch fish, one must change techniques according to the season. Inshore fishing, during the heat of summer, is best early in the morning or late in the evening when the temperature is down. Offshore fishermen, at the same time, know deeper is better because the bottom water temperature is cooler. Everything is temperature dependent, including the fishermen.

So considering the issue of heat, adjust and pace yourself, and avoid the mid-day stroking heat. Inshore fishermen have an advantage by being able to fish the cool morning, zip in during the heat of the day, and then motor out for the evening bite.

Offshore fishermen have a time obstacle regarding the duration of the ride well offshore. How do you avoid the mid-day heater? First, preparation is the key. Proper planning prevents dilly-dallying and saves time. The day or evening before, prep everything you can to go fishing. That includes boat prep and fueling, rod and reel, and tackle considerations, on down to ice and bait. In other words, be sitting on *go* when the boat gets wet. Be ready to hit it quick. That way you can be

114

fishing sooner. Fish when the fishing is best. When the mid-day heat shuts down the bite, roll home. The blow from the boat speed feels great. Besides, you'll be in early enough to steer clear of evening thunderstorms that are sure to occur. It is a win-win.

Adopt the pace of nature; her secret is patience.
Ralph Waldo Emerson

Fish Board

When someone mentions a "fish board," I think of a sheet of marine grade plywood painted slick white with pointy nails or hooks sticking out of it, arranged to best display a fine catch of fish. Without the fish, it looks rather dangerous, kind of medieval. Fish boards normally advertise the marina, its location, and a phone number atop the board in bold lettering. If you have ever been around a marina, you've seen one in person and seen pictures of happy people standing around it with some unhappy fish hanging on it.

Though the title may imply that type of fish board, it is not what the following story is about. Let's go back fishing a couple of weeks ago....

The day started out lucky. Over the past couple of weeks, southerly winds had been pushing the warm, moist air of the Gulf of Mexico over the cooler, dry coastline in the mornings. The mixing of the warm/moist with the cool/dry led to volatile thunder boomers until around midday. Then, in the evening, the typical afternoon storms developed. But this day, the winds were light from the east. Normally, east winds mean trouble, but not this time.

The sky was a happy light blue; the wind was light, and the sea a wind-swelled wobble of one foot or less. Mother Nature had finally put out the Welcome mat.

Catching live bait went better and faster than I expected. Within an hour, a mixture of fifty blue runners, pinfish, pigfish, and a couple cigar minnows filled the tank. Time collecting quality live bait is time well spent.

With the sea state, the cruise speed was up, and the distance seemed down. However, the first three grouper sites only produced one keeper red grouper, thirty-some Florida snapper, and a good kingfish off the flat line. It was good action, but the grouper seemed to be in deeper water, better than sixty-two feet.

There was a wreck in the direction of deeper water, so I decided to give it some fish time. Just for kicks, we trolled a tube lure and a Bomber plug over the wreck first thing. A half a minute after the boat went over the wreck, the rod towing the tube lure was snatched level. I suspected it was a barracuda. However, the fish never jumped, but it was obviously large and strong. After a prolonged and zesty battle amongst the seven fishing coaches, the angler brought the fish boat-side. It was a large amberjack that my cousin and first mate, Tubby, netted aboard. The coaches congratulated the angler and themselves on a most excellent job. It was a team effort of actually one.

Someone peered overboard to notice the entire herd of amberjacks had followed their lost leader to the end. I quickly hooked up a live bait and tossed it out free-line. I didn't have time to hand the pole off before the bait was swallowed. In moments, four people were hooked up on heavy jacks. The limit of six came so fast it was disappointing! While everyone was recounting, I slipped a Nine Pin popper on a big Penn spinner and tossed it out.

"Watch this," I said to draw their attention. A horde of AJs flung themselves on the plug. That set the stage for a thirty minute, post-limit, top-water party where the party pole was shared amongst the crew.

Still needing to put more water underneath the boat, I ran out another twenty-five minutes to deep water. While cruising, some recapped what had just happened, and a couple crashed on the beanbag chairs.

The bottom machine lit up when the boat passed over the waypoint before anchoring. *Hotdog! Good grouper,* I said to myself.

When the boat became taut on the rode, six baits rained down. For the first two to three minutes…nothing. Then, three poles were yanked down, hard. Two of the three broke off. My immediate thought was…the fish that escaped are going to sound the "gong" and kill the bite. The third fish came aboard and changed my mind. It was a twelve-pound-plus, genuine American red snapper (ARS). Everyone celebrated but Tubby and me.

The ARS was out of season. I dropped the law bomb. They took some photos, and then I tried to explain a crazy regulation to another crew for the umpteenth time.

117

The next half hour was, what could have been, an ARS blast. I stopped the fishing after one ARS floated off, even after a good venting. We luckily picked up two gag grouper on the free lines during that period. However, I'm not one to kill one type of fish in hopes of catching another. We had to leave. Honestly, everyone agreed with my call. There are very few unscrupulous anglers relative to the law breaking "fish hogs," yet rules are set for those who would misuse them. I should be allowed to collect the dead ARS as by-catch in lieu of letting them float to waste. The adage, "The sharks need to eat," is an excuse for those few people who aren't trustworthy and who need policing. Anyway, we left.

At one spot, which turned out to be our last, someone noticed the flash of "chicken" dolphin around the boat. Usually, I have a jig-ready pole for just such an occasion, but I was ill prepared. I tossed some bits and pieces of squid and fish overboard to entice the dolphin back and hurried myself, tying on a twenty-pound leader and a bargain bin dollar-ninety-nine spoon—picked up at Bass Pro—to a trout spin combo. Also, I prepped two other combos with a single 1/0 hook for free lining cut bait.

I was twisting a rig together when someone asked, "Captain, what is that?"

"Probably a turtle," I replied without looking.

"No, it's not a turtle," was the response I looked around and was finger guided to the object. It was as large as a turtle but not a turtle. It was close off the stern. I put one and one together. One, the sighting of dolphin and two, floating debris attracts dolphin. I came up with a brainstorm to weigh anchor and check it out.

The floating object was a well-weathered board, three by five feet. It was being homesteaded by a hundred dolphin or more. The board was lit up, flashing neon underneath like a street showboat low-rider. The cast went out before my command to go. The show was on in leaping splendor. All wanted a fishing pole, but there were only three ready for action. I grabbed some extra poles to rig up. Tubby was cutting bait, picking up fish flopping on the deck, and running around doing something else important at the moment. I was handing out freshly rigged rods and re-rigging those that had been broke-off.

The school had jumped off the board and followed the boat. It was a racket of fish. Blood skids were on both sides of the boat and on the bow. A cutting board full of fresh fish strips lasted less time than a sushi plate in front of a group of enthusiastic patrons.

"How many?" I asked Tubby.

He shrugged telling me he had no idea. We had bailed over a good number of dolphin in a quick forty minutes. I was thinking we had taken enough, including three for my family.

There is no need to catch the legal limit to have the most fun—enough is enough. The dolphin limit is ten per person or sixty per vessel, but I'm not one to over fish anything. I'd rather take in a diverse box of fish than one filled with only one species. The diversity attitude is not solely based on conservation. Rather, fishing is supposed to be entertaining, and the best entertainment comes in variety, thinking in terms of fish, as well as, technique. We had a lot of fun and collected a bunch of fish doing so. It was time to move on; actually it was time to return to Steinhatchee. We all enjoyed the offshore fish board more than the fish board at River Haven Marina, pinning down the amberjack, grouper, kingfish, and twenty-two dolphin.

I marvel how the fishes live in the sea.
William Shakespeare

Oh No

The forecast from the evening before didn't play out. By six am it had bumped up an extra foot or two. I'm not a morning person. Foggy-headed me had to change from plan A of last night to plan B early in the morning. In the hazy mind of slumber, I re-read the NOAA forecast, local forecast, looked at the Doppler readings, and peaked a view from the non-lying sea buoy stationed one hundred miles off Pensacola.

I was waiting on an epiphany while in my one seat library, but I think you have to be somewhat awake to have one. So I bumbled through the rest of my morning habits, thankful that Casey took care of the details of putting our necessities in the truck, even driving to River Haven Marina. There, I found myself going through the routine of putting the fishing poles together, still in a fog about where and how I was going to fish that day.

It was an important day to be wrapped around Colby. Colby was a ten-year-old, avid fisherman. His dad, Brad, told me he could get the boy up before daybreak, fish into the late evening, and when told they had to go home, Colby would ask for ten more minutes. I could relate; I was the same way. As a matter of fact, if age hadn't caught up with this "Peter Pan," I'd still be the same way. I remember never feeling the aches and pains from the day before. Youth is wasted on the young.

The rest of the crew included Colby's mom, Shannon. She was a fun-loving woman who enjoyed fishing and being outside in general. Christine was Colby's fourteen-year-old sister. She was basically there for the ride. Young teens are often aloof. Twenty-five miles offshore, Brad disclosed privately she was a little put-off by not being able to text friends. Apparently, the young lady was lost-at-sea without her iPhone. Forced precious moments with the family…OMG!

Anyway, Colby was shy first thing in the morning, but as his dad told me, he soon got over it. The first stop was to collect fresh live-bait—a lightweight combo with a hair-hook, bream—baited with a tidbit of squid and enough of a sinker to let it skim across the top of the grass bed. This simple rig was the undoing of sixty or so pinfish and pigfish. The bait well was loaded to the brim with live-bait; pardon the pun. Brad said we could do this all day, and Colby would be happy. But I wasn't happy with that idea. I wanted the boy to have a fish-ripping time and to let him encounter some of the big fish and big fun he had been reading about on my website.

However, during bait collection, I still found myself in a blur as to what to do that day. Casey made a suggestion to me on the side. It was the epiphany I was looking for.

The first stop was a small, shallow water ledge north of Steinhatchee. I hadn't stopped there in two years or more. I had no feeling, no little voice in my head. I just knew by the forecast that the best ride out was in a northerly direction, because the best ride in would be southerly.

We anchored just above the break, and I put two live baits off the stern. Casey put two weighted baits off amidships. It took a few minutes before the starboard stern free-line bait behaved like it needed a Prozac. The pole doubled, and the line screamed away. I handed the pole to Brad, and after a ten-minute bit of cockpit chaos, Casey gaffed a good twenty pound king for Brad–that was cool.

During that forty-minute anchorage, Shannon and Brad boated three keeper gag grouper, two shorts, and two rocked-up. Then the action stopped.

We moved to a place I named Train Wreck. There are no boxcars down there, but I've been schooled and spooled enough that it warrants the name. It is one of those places where it's hot or it's not. That day, except for the run off from a fine kingfish, it was not. Within a half hour, we moved eleven miles west.

The first two stops were duds in terms of grouper. However, I had time to introduce Colby to the wonderful world of Florida snapper, also known as pink mouth grunts. A knocker rig with squid on a trout outfit was Colby's passport to self-stardom. After a couple of minor goofs, I told Colby to let the bait hit the bottom, count to five, and yank.

That small piece of advice led him to proclaim, "I only made it to three." He was his own legend, loading the cooler for the family.

A kid in the throes of catching fish is far better than catching any one fish yourself. Their joy of fishing is infectious for the entire boat. I know that because it is one of the prime reasons I keep fishing.

Anyway, during the course of the next couple hours, everybody, including his sunbathing sister, had rolled up a grouper. Most of the grouper were short of legal, but some were unnecessary to measure. I wanted Colby to reel in a good gag grouper.

I anchored on the edge of a four-foot lime rock relief; it showed a sparkle of fish on the sonar as we passed over. My little voice said, "This is Colby's spot." Casey threw the anchor over. We came to rest perfectly. Fresh live baits were sent down. I hooked up and handed the rod to Brad. He invited Christine to help him. Shannon was the next to help Brad. The fish were active below us.

Colby was rolling up the Florida snapper to my right on the portside. His line was up when I hooked up on a grouper. I got the grouper ten feet off the bottom and turned to Colby and said, "Come here"! The pole was well bent over in my hands when I said that. I looked dead at him when he didn't take action quickly.

He was slowly back stepping away from me when he said, "Oh No."

I was confused by the retort from the avid young fishing dude. Perplexed, my face and mouth said, "No, what?"

Then Colby spit out, "No sir."

I was stymied. His unexpected response and then with manners froze my mind. I had no comeback; I was TKO'd by a small boy on my own boat! Judging by the silence, everyone else was momentarily taken back as well.

I put a few more turns on the reel and gave it over to Brad. He reeled up a good grouper.

Colby took many lighthearted cracks from all aboard after that incident. His sister was tenacious, as older sisters tend to pick-up the "opportunity ball" and run as far as they can with it. She reminded him over and over and over that she had caught a grouper. She wasn't scared.

Inspired by humiliation, Colby bucked-up and brought in three grouper with the help of his dad. By doing so, he somewhat redeemed himself, especially in his own eyes, but not to his sister.

On the ride in, Colby reminded everyone he still caught the most fish. Don Quixote Colby rode the fiberglass pony back to Steinhatchee in his own glory.

A day of fishing is as good as you let it become.
Salty Dog

The Drop

It was the fortuitous blend of fate tethered to excessive hours of dull-mindedly viewing the bottom machine screen, while underway from one waypoint to the next, which allowed me a side glimpse of a little piece of marine heaven. I mashed "mark" on the GPS, slowed down, and turned back for a fresh look. Was I having a fish fantasy vision, or did I fumble over a "fish bomb?" I zigzagged around where I had marked until the sand bottom firmed to hard rock bottom with an electronic show of blue balls hovering above it. The UFOs, unidentified fish objects, were most likely gag grouper. I double marked the spot and scratched the address down on a beat up notebook, my black book of numbers with fish symbols in lieu of stars for a good time. This new address was marked with a question mark.

I wanted to check it out, but we already had a good catch and were running half an hour behind. It is not that a clock dictates me; I haven't owned a watch in over twenty-five years. But the boat cleaning was going to be pushed into the twilight hours when the no-see-ums are at their best and worst. Relative to size, no-see-ums have to be one of the strongest critters on earth. They can not only move creatures billions of times their mass, but they also put them out of their minds while doing it! Anyway, that new number was going to be checked out first, second, or whenever the next day.

While riding in, I got to thinking about where I found that new piece of potential loving. I took into account that there is nothing new to find. It is too late to be Christopher Columbus, Ponce de Leon, or Lewis and Clark because of all of the commercial fishermen and recreational anglers before me. But sometimes, a storm or winter pulls the sand blanket off the rocks, and fresh, old, good bottom reappears that has been asleep for a while. I had traveled across that area many times only to observe lots of sand. Maybe this particular course was a wee bit different, and I picked up the needle in the haystack. Whatever...I was anxious to hit that *gag spot* sometime the next day.

Six nice fellows, who had fished with me before, arrived at the dock early, thirty minutes before shove-off. Not being a morning person, I readily accepted their offer to help tote stuff to dress the boat. Some folks are too proud for that; I just know pride goes before a fall. In the early morning, I may be prone to a gravity storm and end up wet off the dock. Besides, the joy is in the journey, so start it early, given the knock of opportunity.

The weather pattern had remained steady; the course we took the last morning was still boat-rider friendly. Besides, the day before, we caught well in that direction. Furthermore, I overlooked waypoints I didn't have time to tap, and, best of all for me, the new hole lay in that direction, perhaps the one that could be the best for the day.

The mate, with additional volunteer hands, prepped the boat quickly. My foggy morning guidance didn't come into play, as if Garrett needed my input in the first place. We broke away early, happy not to feed the flying teeth any longer than necessary. However, the mass swarm crawling in my hair broke me forty yards before making the "Resume Safe Speed" sign. I yelped notice to all and pushed the throttles forward, blowing those flying teeth out of our hair using mechanically generated wind. Sticking my head out from the helm to catch the flowing air, I ran my fingers through my hair in a "bye-bye" fluff wave to the bugs that was far more genuine than flight attendants use toward disembarking passengers.

I broke away from the channel after passing the #8 marker and ran a mile or so to a patch of deeper grass bottom displayed on my e-box water TV, sonar, as a thick, loose, red-colored bottom cover. Trout rods were handed out to five of six anglers rigged with #12 long shank pinfish hooks tapped with an eighth ounce split shot squeezed a foot and a half above the hook. The previous day's belly meat cut in tiny strips quickly paid the livewell bill for a fresh, hundred count of pinfish, pigfish, and other miscellaneous lively grouper getters in three slow drifts.

I couldn't resist the pull of my new Columbus waypoint. Maybe the boat pulled itself toward the new bottom without my helm control like a horse trotting back to its barn. The anchor splashed water on those standing starboard. The rode tightened well over the show of the day before. I was a kid waiting on Santa Claus while Garrett placed the

125

sardine and pinfish cookies out. The first two baits hit the bottom, maybe before their poles bent over double. It was on like *Donkey Kong*. Garrett and I baited the next two hooks with gaffs in the other hand. The last two anglers had frozen fish sticks tossed towards them on the deck. "Go with it!" They joined in.

Though Garrett and I were working as fast as flash, de-hooking fish and re-baiting hooks, the action was too much. It broke down when one of the guys got broke-off. I handed him an extra rod and reel combo, but I had to dropout to re-rig after another man got broke-off. It turned into a self-serve situation that nobody minded at all. Garrett and I glanced at each other a couple of times with faces of disbelief.

Every gag brought across the gunnels I eye-measured to be well over the minimum measurement of twenty-two inches. We thought we tossed seventeen in the fish box. In the chaos, we timely released thirteen fish on deck. Four guys had a fish in hand. Garrett and I conversed but didn't come to an agreement on the exact number of fish. We had lost count. At that time, the law allowed five grouper per angler. Garrett hastily rooted around the fish-box double confirming the first seventeen in the box. That number was marked by pencil strokes on the lid. We released the fresh four the guys were holding. I stopped the other two fishermen in the process of dropping down more bait to the bottom.

All this happened in forty-five minutes. "The drop"–every fisherman dreams of being there when it happens. It was a bite from yester-year. It was a bite I wish everybody I take fishing could be a part of. It has happened here and there afterwards, yet it is always exceptional.

Those encounters propel us outdoorsmen and well-admired, respected outdoorswomen to seek more exciting encounters of fin or fur during our lifetimes. The joy is in the journey. Isn't it?

I know of no optimism so great as that, which perennially blooms in the heart of a fisherman.
Burton L. Spiller

Turducken

Turducken is a rather odd title for a fishing story. When most of us hear the word Turducken, we think of the Thanksgiving Cajun creation where a raw deboned chicken is stuffed in a raw deboned duck, and that deboned double is jostled into a raw deboned turkey. Ironically, stuffing is layered between each bird. It is either baked or fried to a state of perfection. You'll wish your stomach were Turducken sized once you taste it and add in the mashed taters 'n gravy, green bean casserole, collards, sweet taters, corn pudding, home-made breads, cranberry sauce, and the other family traditional foods. Afterwards, no one can resist cutting into the displayed pumpkin, apple, and chocolate pies folks bring to the feast. Then, slow Aunt Clara finally gets around to unveiling her super-rich homemade pecan pie. Everyone is obligated to have a slice. Now you're Turducken stuffed, down for the count.

The self-imposed bellyache is followed by a prolonged group nap. We've all done the Thanksgiving turkey nap at our house or someone else's. It's also a tradition that the football game watches us for at least two quarters.

Anyway, back to Turducken in terms of fishing. This has happened so often over the years I was forced to name it. I came up with, obviously, Turducken. I also realize I'm not the first to encounter the situation.

***

Join us on the boat.

We picked up a lively livewell of bait first thing in the morning from the traps. The bait well was full of pinfish and pigfish. We cruised offshore. We eventually found ourselves over an amberjack spot.

Amberjack love hanging out around anything with relief off the bottom whether natural, such as a large rock formation or artificial, such as a wreck or offshore tower. What draws the amberjack to these locations is an abundance of food. Baitfish of all types swarm around the structure because it offers more protection than open water. The congregation of baitfish makes the spots "fish kitchens." In the Steinhatchee area, the kitchen accommodates other fish such as red snapper, mangrove snapper, grouper, kingfish, barracuda, cobia, sharks and others, such as jewfish (PC goliath grouper).

Every amberjack spot I know of, and even those I don't know, have resident jewfish. I'd bet the farm on that. Their job in life is to grow Goliath by eating anything and everything that wants to hang out where they reside, sharks included. Jewfish can grow to over one thousand pounds; that's half a ton! There are some jewfish that swim inside the wheelhouse of a wreck in their youth and eat so much they imprison themselves there.

So we were anchored over a kitchen, a wreck. The ingredients were aligned above and below. Those ingredients were raw pinfish above, and raw amberjack with jewfish below. It was time to start preparing the Turducken.

I started with a large spinning combination with appropriate size line, leader, and hook; thirty pound test Trilene Big Game in green, sixty pound Trilene Big Game in clear, and a Mustad 9174 6/0, respectively. Then, I selected a fresh caught, large pinfish from the livewell and free-lined that ingredient off the stern into the large bowl of hot water called the Gulf of Mexico. I set the fishing rod stir-stick in a holder. The pinfish seductively wiggled to draw an amberjack to a boil. When the stir-stick bent over double, it indicated the pinfish was done. Collectively, thirteen-year-old Jimmy was coaxed over. I, the chef, handed him the stir-stick. Jimmy was a newbie or, for the purpose of this story, a sous-chef…a Japanese word for a chef in training.

The sous-chef was struggling longer than usual with the initial part of the recipe as compared to a more seasoned offshore fish chef. I, the chef, was at his side, giving advice, "Pull up gently and stir down quickly." The hooked amberjack with the pinfish stuffed in its belly was cooking about wildly with a bunch of his friends trailing him.

The resident food critic, a jewfish, sensed something different was cooking in the kitchen above and rose to see if there was a new item on the menu. Its large form was no secret when we saw it enter the kitchen

128

from the boat. It was obvious that critic had eaten a lot of samples. Seeing a gang of crazed amberjacks running around the kitchen, the critic had to be thinking, "It must be great; they're wild about it." The critic was suspended motionless watching the action, figuring out which amberjack had the new menu item. When the rambunctious, stuffed amberjack swam by too close, the critic swallowed it whole with the treat inside it. Jimmy unknowingly watched the making of his first Turducken; a pinfish stuffed inside an amberjack that was now stuffed inside a jewfish.

"Jimmy, you got yourself a Turducken," I said.

He had no idea what I meant. His confidence was elevated by his self-perceived semi-success from his first piscatorial culinary creation. He began to wage war against his over-sized food critic. The food critic didn't even realize it had engaged in so much as an oral disagreement. It went back down to take a nap after feasting. The sous-chef angler bellyached when his line collapsed.

He had nothing to do with stuffing the pinfish in the amberjack and no idea about stuffing a chicken in a duck. He lucked out, being in the kitchen when it all came together inside a Jewish-turkey. Game over...we all needed to take a nap after an obligatory slice of Aunt Clara's rich humble pie.

Sometimes you got to learn to suck it up; then take a nap.
Salty Dog

Claude

The anchor line came taut above a mixed pile of stuff that somehow rose from below or fell from above to give relief to an otherwise flat, sandy bottom some time ago. It was an area of sparse natural lime rock that had been amended with additional debris to make a cluster of artificial reefs. That day the water was top-to-bottom clear. The reef was easily distinguishable from the boat as semi-large, dark patches blotting the white sand twenty-some feet below. The reef appeared shadowy due to the marine flora and fauna attached and growing on the hard substrate. Peering overboard, we noticed small, thin, black lines milling about the fixed black patches. The more we looked, the more we noticed a lot more black lines wiggling about the littered bottom.

"Do you see them?" I asked.

Casey, our mate said, "Captain there's a load of fish down there; are you picking them up on the sonar?"

The bottom machine was sprinkled with fish hovering ten feet above and on down to bottom. The sheepshead were in full spawn over the jumbled bottom.

John held his Claude on the gunnel so he could see the fish below.

Claude said excitedly, "I can see fish Daddy."

Apparently, Claude misunderstood that was the sole reason he was propped up on the gunnel, because he took that opportunity to unzip and fire off a long strafing round before anyone could do anything. I noticed the distance and told John, "The boy's got pressure."

John laughed, but Brenda, the mother seemed embarrassed.

"Don't worry about it Brenda; the fish appreciate the warmth," I said to lighten the moment.

It was late winter, early spring in North Florida.

Casey busied himself making sheepshead chow by chopping two

pounds of frozen shrimp into one inch to inch-and-a-half sized pieces. He put the diced shrimp into a large plastic bowl, added a splash of seawater, and sprinkled in some ice to keep the bait fresh. Bait, like seafood is always best served fresh. Casey placed the bait bowl atop the flat surface of the large fish box under the captain's bench seat with a wet towel wrapped around the base to secure it during cruising. The bait was accessible yet out of the way. From experience, we both knew once the bite was "on," there would be little time to cut bait. Sheepshead fishing can be so fast that the slowest link in the catching chain is taking the fish off the hook and/or re-baiting.

Casey was dealing with the bait. The Tirey family was caught up watching the live fish show nearby and below us. During that time, I collected six, lightweight trout combos. There were only three to four of us fishing at a time, but the extra backup outfits were necessary to keep the action reeling when a line was cut or broken. No need to wait for a pole to be re-rigged; just hand out another one ready to go.

A hyper sheepshead on a trout rod is a worthy adversary to a well-salted angler. Fishing is supposed to be fun. The fun of any fish is in the fight.

The trout poles Casey rigged up were spooled with ten-pound test main line joined to an eighteen-inch section of thirty-pound test leader using a double uni-knot.

Don't use a swivel to connect the lines because it adds unnecessary weight. Besides, the function of a swivel is to prevent line twist not an excuse to learn the proper knot.

The lightweight outfits also increase sensitivity. Sensitivity is a very important aspect of successful sheepshead fishing. You can literally watch a ten-pound sheepshead eat your bait and not feel it happen. It is said you have to set the hook before you feel the bite. Actually, with your forefinger on the line, the bite feels like the slight tap of a live oak leaf falling in the palm of your hand.

To the end of the leader Casey tied a light eighth-ounce jig head. The most common size around here, Steinhatchee, is quarter ounce. I haven't noticed the color of the jig head to be important. Pick whatever paint-job makes you most confident. However, the weight is important. You want your bait to spend as much time as possible in the water column amongst the fish so to be more noticed. Choosing an excessively heavy weight or jig head takes your bait through the fish like a bullet to the bottom.

131

Now, eventually, a fish may root around and discover your bait, but it is far better to advertise it slowly through the fish, so they'll notice then follow your bait and take it on the drop. Furthermore, sheepshead prefer to spawn over bottom that is an entangling hook magnetic jungle such that if your bait spends much time there, you'll find yourself wasting time attached to the bottom rather than the fish. Consequently, you end up losing and leaving dollars below and behind. Avoid wasting valuable time and tackle by adjusting the rig to conditions.

Proper anchoring is more important to successful sheepshead fishing than having the best bait. The boat has to be positioned very well to present the bait to the fish. Remember, they are spawning, so they are more interested in sex than food. The fish aren't prone to go for take-out but will accept delivery. Therefore, if you so much as sense you are not anchored right, you're not anchored right. Always take whatever time or effort it takes to anchor well. In doing so, you will catch more sheepshead, or any other fish for that matter. Promise. Always do things as well as you possibly can.

While I was growing up, my dad told me to always continue with whatever job I was doing until it was done well. I few times I didn't do as well as he instructed. Those belt straps still encourage me to re-anchor until it is done well, and it has improved my fishing as well as other matters in my life.

There are no two days alike; it boils down to starting with an educated guess and adjusting to the situation at hand. In terms of sinkers or jig heads, use the least amount of weight necessary to keep the bait where the fish are hanging out without getting hung up. For example, if the current is fairly strong, an up current cast with a quarter-ounce or more jig head is necessary to present your bait where the fish are. If the current is slack, simply pin the shrimp bit on a 1/0 hook and let it drift down naturally. Watch where the line enters the water, and when you notice a twitch, set the hook quickly! In our case, Casey picked the eighth-ounce jig head, glancing at the situation. If his choice were incorrect, it would be nothing more than a nip of a knot and a re-tie to readjust. Casey's educated situational eighth-ounce jig head guess was spot-on.

While Casey was cutting bait, he was pushing some of the smaller bits and pieces to the side. I grabbed up a couple of handfuls of shrimp scraps and tossed them off the bow. The current was weak. The bits of shrimp softly rained down while slowly carried aft in the slight current.

Brenda asked, "What are you doing?"

I replied, "At my restaurant, I give away complimentary appetizers."

I smiled and told her it got the bite going quicker, like smelling coffee and bacon in the morning.

She smiled back with new understanding.

"Claude, you better get ready," she said.

"Mommy the fish are eating the shrimp Captain Brian threw away."

"Big little man, are you ready to catch one of those sheepshead?" Casey courted Claude.

"You bet Casey," was Claude's excited reply; but he didn't pee this time.

"Now watch the pretty, pink jig head," Casey coached.

With that, Casey tossed the bait slightly forward, and we all watched the small jig parachute down. When the bait was just astern, about twelve feet below, a buck sheepshead darted over, looked at it, and then pecked it. Casey set the hook. The pole arched over. The fish flashed around recklessly.

"Here you go Claude; here you go," Casey spoke to Claude while handing him the pole.

Casey handed Claude the pole but maintained a grip about mid-way up the rod. Claude knew the function of the reel handle. That is the part of the reel you turn round and round to bring the fish in. Casey had to talk the youngster down, so he'd gather some understanding of the reel drag.

"When I raise the pole up, you don't reel. When I lower the pole down, reel. OK Claude?" Casey quickly stated.

Claude agreed with everything Casey said yet reeled continuously even after I slid the net under the fish. We had to physically stop him like *Forrest Gump* running through the end zone.

"Reel, Claude, Reel!" If everybody in this world could get half as happy, once a week, as Claude was in that moment, we'd be looking forward to living, and there would be no suicide.

Brenda thoroughly digitally video documented proof, it took more help from Casey, me, his father, and three fish later before it began to click in Claude's head. The fishing line was collected on the down stroke. Claude was the star of the boat show for the first *Look-at-me*

133

Times.

"Casey and Claude are working well together. Are ya'll ready to join in?" I asked the parents.

John was more than ready. Brenda was hesitantly willing to give it a try.

"Is this my pole," John asked, pointing to one of the trout rods in the rocket launcher behind the captain's bench.

"Sure, go for it," I replied. John pinned on a chunk of shrimp and was off to the races. I baited a pole for Brenda. The boys were fishing on the port side. Brenda and I took to the starboard. I showed her how to cast. She was a natural. She intently watched the bait and set the hook at the perfect moment. She hooted and laughed like she just hit the lotto every time she reeled in a fish. On the other hand, or I should say on the other side, John was frustrated at missing the fish he watched take his bait. His bait to hook up ratio was shrimp-expensive.

"John, you have to set the hook just before you feel the bite," Casey told him.

John responded with a despondent look.

Brenda responded by saying, "It is easy honey. Just set the hook when you see the fish eat the shrimp."

That was a splash of saltwater in John's open ego.

Casey and Claude tag teamed up a big female sheepshead. I went and got the net for her arrival on deck. The fish was a bit over ten pounds and so pregnant the struggle had caused eggs to ooze from her vent. It was time for a biology lesson since I had Claude's full attention. He was gawking at the largest fish he'd ever caught.

"Claude, this big sheepshead is the mommy of a million babies. She is releasing some of her babies now," I pointed out the eggs dripping from her. "We have to make a very important choice in the next minute. We can put her in the fish box so you can have a dinner, or we can put her back in the ocean, so she can make more sheepshead to catch next year. What would you like to do?" I asked.

It was obvious I had posed a great moral dilemma on a young boy. Do I kill the babies by keeping the mother of the biggest fish of my life? Or do I deny myself and give them all away?

After a hard moment of contemplation, "Captain Brian, that is the biggest fish I've ever caught in my life, but my mommy has a picture of it, and I want this mommy to go home," Claude said in the purity of a child unbiased by the greed of the world. He helped me release her.

"Captain, I named that mommy fish Molly after my cat," Claude announced unexpectedly.

"Why did you name the fish after your cat?" I asked.

"Because she had a lot of babies before Mommy and Daddy had the doctor put her in 'neutral'?"

That statement made the day. After that, it didn't take long before fifteen, medium-sized sheepshead were on ice. There were a lot of catch and release of the extra small and large during that time. Even John managed to put three fish in the cooler, all by himself.

Five fish per angler is my boat limit, a third the legal limit. When any fish is spawning, it is best to apply common sense, not necessarily fish regulations because what you're taking isn't just for today but also from the future. Tomorrow's children should have the opportunity to experience the fun we were having in the here and now. What is wrong with making it better than when it used to be?

"How about doing something different for a while," I said to all. The Tireys, in agreement, wanted to find out what else I had in my bag of fish tricks using fish sticks. While things were getting back in order and snack time was going on, I told Casey I'd like to do some near-shore grouper trolling. We readied four trolling rods before pulling the anchor. Two to three miles southwest were scattered rocky patches. Historically, it was a great time to troll. Hopefully, it would work out well. In the back of my mind, I didn't want Claude to get bored. Fishing is supposed to be fun, especially for children.

After a brief run down on the how tos of trolling, we four adults put out four Rapala plugs staggered to run relatively shallow to deep. The water clarity was close to pure. We could see the rocky live bottom below as dark blotches, sometimes isolated pieces, at other times as linear or mosaic patterns. The temperature was in the low to mid-sixties. The grouper should be active.

I started at one of the best areas simply to give myself an idea if trolling was going to pan out. Again, I didn't want to bore a child with too much inactivity. Ten seconds after running over the first cluster of rocks, we got lucky. Two of the four poles bent over. The game was on. Casey helped Claude with the first pole that got hit. John grabbed the second strike. Brenda and I hurriedly reeled in the two blank plugs. I was racing to beat Claude in. After stowing my rod away and asking Brenda to carry her pole forward, I handed Casey a gaff for his fish and took another gaff to help John. As luck would have it, both gag grouper

135

were keepers. I was one happy captain. Casey and Claude were captured on digital film many times before we began trolling again. John and I were photographed as well.

In two hours of trolling, we boxed seven keeper grouper and a few throwbacks. One of the grouper was a touch over twelve pounds and Claude reeled it in with help from his dad.

"Casey, how big is this fish?" Claude asked.

"Oh, it's twelve or thirteen pounds," Casey replied.

"Captain, this fish is bigger than the mama sheepshead!" exclaimed Claude.

"Claude, I think you had that one coming," I told him with a smile that wrapped around my head. Brenda took pictures of John holding the fish above Claude's head like it was the Sugar Bowl trophy.

We finished the day dabbling with some ravenous sea bass on the same trout poles we caught the sheepshead.

There is nothing like watching a child catch a fish every time he or she drops bait. A child will turn self-professional at anything within minutes given enough fanfare. Claude was putting sea bass in his and our trophy Sugar Bowl cooler.

When we docked the boat, Casey had the fish box lid open at Claude's request. I glanced at it, and it looked good to me too. Claude disembarked and made it his mission to inform everybody at the marina how good his day was. You can't buy advertisement like that anywhere, and the cost was priceless.

Some men brought two large coolers of sheepshead to the fish-cleaning table. They flipped the lids open and started tossing some of the fish up on the table. I was standing close by watching.

Claude ran from behind me; he took a long, somber look and blurted out loud, "Mister that big one was a mommy; why didn't you let her have her babies?"

The man about to clean fish glanced at little Claude, then he and I locked eyes, he noticed the others around awaiting a response, and then he continued putting fish on the cleaning table without saying a word. The lack of an answer from the big man meant the man inside was provoked...hopefully to contemplation.

Ignorant men don't know what good they hold in their hands until they've flung it away.
Sophocles (c. 495-406 B.C..)

To Feel Something

There was a chop on the water inside the protection of the Steinhatchee River. A light spritz from port and from bow was already glazing the Plexiglas windshield. As we exited the river mouth, I looked forward into the Gulf of Mexico and saw elephants dancing on the horizon. The waves near shore were white capped, two to three-foot dance steps, as non-rhythmic as old white men trying to do "the Hustle" at a wedding reception. The waves were the result of swirling, sucking winds trailing the prior day's cold front. The Gulf was a washtub that would only get more agitated the more boat lengths traveled westward offshore.

I was paying attention to my little voice. The national marine forecast has no little voice. The sea-time experience of common sense, shouting in my head, was more firmly stuck than the dried ink stamped parchment on which the United States government approved my captain license.

Even though my Twin Vee thirty-two foot catamaran would make the trip safely and more comfortably than other comparable vessels of greater size, it was still a center console with no plastic water shields. The conditions were such that there would be much uncomfortable movement and spray-like-rain for the long ride.

My guests were from and around Atlanta, Georgia. Larry and his wife, Linda, lived in suburbia just outside Atlanta, still inside the urban sprawl. Larry was a civil engineer in the administrative department of a large company working in contracts with the DOT. Linda was a homemaker with four kids, one of whom was Larry. Tim—Larry's brother—and his wife Ann lived in a small town well north of Atlanta. He worked at the local Post Office for twenty plus years. Ann drove a school bus and was likewise a homemaker for their five kids and Tim. Felix and his wife Fran—Larry and Tim's father and mother—lived in the same small town as Tim and Ann. They were semi-retired. Felix had worked thirty-some years at the local paper mill. Fran raised six boys on Felix's pay, budgeted the money, fed the chickens and pigs on scraps and odds and ends, put up the meat after slaughter, helped in their large garden, canned vegetables for winter, as well as babysat, made jellies, pies and cakes, and mended clothes for extra cash.

She smiled telling me, "That was when a half-a-dollar was worth something."

Fran reminded me of what my mom, Dixie, had done for Dad and me, with his Army, then Post Office paycheck. Fran brought my thoughts further back in time to when my Mawmaw (grandmother) took mom and me in while Dad was serving duty in Korea. She loved Mom and me in her home. Her home used to be a railroad depot. It was floated on a barge down the New River and set on river stones in Montgomery, West Virginia. She had taken care of Pawpaw and their ten offspring on a coal miner's pay there. Mawmaw did the same things Fran did and had a quilting frame hung above her feather bed. I could relate, in my relative history, with Fran.

Women are awesome yet unacknowledged most of the time. Count me in the deadwood club idiot pile of men-folk; I'm sorry for not buying flowers and such or just taking the right time to acknowledge my wife Gina. Gina, I love you; thanks for putting up with me.

Larry and Tim arrived at the dock early enough to see Jake and me dressing up the boat. They asked if they could help carry down rods and so forth. It was helpful. I've learned not to turn down volunteers, especially in the morning. I've never been a morning person; I'll always appreciate any help I can get early of the morning.

Felix and the ladies came down around seven o'clock. We loaded up their belongings, shoving-off after a couple precautionary potty breaks.

Upon exiting the river mouth and seeing the snotty sea conditions, I shifted to plan B. Thankfully, my boat was adaptable. I had the thirteen minutes needed to get to the bait trap to develop plan B. I had to do B while engaged in conversation. Did I mention not being a morning person?

While everyone was occupied watching Jake work the bait trap, my mind was spinning something together. Doable options were jigging for trout on the relatively smooth grass flats and near-shore or shallow trolling for grouper, kingfish, and Spanish mackerel.

138

Additionally, anchoring on some high relief spots to free-line live and dead baits for whatever was a viable option. Then pushing out, when conditions permitted, to do a Florida Snapper/Sea Bass cooler jam would work as well.

This would be quite a bit different than the grouper/red snapper trip they had planned on. Furthermore, plan B might require a charter discount, and nowadays, in the for-hire charter business, discounts hurt more than yester years.

Jake had just finished up the bait business and reset the trap.

I announced, "Folks, the weatherman fibbed again; sea conditions are going to be rough till at least noon when the air and water temperatures equilibrate. I believe ya'll would enjoy a bit of near shore action until things "pretty-off" after noon."

Larry, the oldest son, said, "We just want to have some fun."

Ann chirped in, "I don't want to get sick."

Fran, who was sitting beside me on the captain's bench, gave me the female look of approval for me not wanting to bounce us offshore.

Felix walked around the cockpit, put his right hand around my neck and shoulders and said, "Captain, I just want everybody to have a good time, and we don't really care about the fish." Looking into his eyes gave more testimony than his hand on a Bible.

I was off the hook in terms of needing to run offshore. Now I had the pleasure of exercising the fishing skills I learned before charting for a living and teaching those skills to others. Not that going offshore, dropping bait to the bottom, and pulling up grouper isn't fun, but the challenge of finding fish and catching them in the shallows is the thrill for me. The foul weather presented me a challenge, a good thing.

I maneuvered the boat up wind to drift across the patchy bottom the bait trap was set on. Most of the trout poles we carry onboard were pre-rigged with jig heads. The couple that weren't, Jake rigged ready while on the move.

People who think they are saving money by not having a mate onboard are saving quarters for their dollars. Time offshore is expensive, trust me, and a good mate, the only ones that roll with me, save time and cash for all—thought from a captain.

For an hour, we drifted back and across the patchy bottom. During which time we picked up two legal-sized trout, one flounder, and some seabass. We also caught a gracious plenty of short trout, were pestered

139

with throw-back lizardfish, and were cut off several times by Spanish or small sharks. The action kept steady which was a good thing.

That was enough time spent doing that, at least for me. While they were busy on the drift, I rigged up four trolling rods running shallow plugs ready for grouper, kingfish, Spanish mackerel, or whatever. I wanted them to get a big fix of fishing. I needed a fix as well.

Even though the conditions were a bit sloppy, the boat could run in a straight-line, so four trolling outfits could be set out without making a hundred-foot, tangled, monofilament scarf. I hadn't noticed much floating grass while we were trout fishing. Floating grass, large mats, or windrows, can make trolling a miserable act of raking grass off saltwater with lures, a non-option. But this day the water was clean, allowing us to run four lines back without hassle.

The aft lines pulled plugs that skirted the shallow bottom. The forward lines dragged one, red and white, two-ounce jig and a medium-sized Clarke spoon. I was trying to cover the water column with the spread to target grouper to mackerel. The troll was semi-downwind for comfort. I zigzagged to put the spread over as much hard bottom as possible.

We picked up two nice gag grouper, three shorts, and one snake kingfish, but Jake and I noticed there was an ample supply of Spanish mackerel that were popping the lures often. I decided to switch the spread to four Floreo jigs with six inches of #2 wire leader. It worked so well, trolling was no longer necessary. We gave Felix, Tim, Larry, and Linda the lightweight rods we used trolling to cast randomly on the leeward side. Fran and Ann weren't casters, so we pitched out jigs with cut bait under corks on the windward side. The waves gave the jigs action. The cut-bait scent with the cork was something they could watch to tell when a fish took the bait. The Spanish were in a swarm. Everyone caught fish.

Fran didn't have a clue as to how to fish, what she was doing, or when to reel, but she had the most fun of all. She sat on a cooler watching and cheering as others brought in fish and went Christmas morning kid happy when a fish took her bait. Fran was alive. The reel drags squealed, and some fish were lost or cut-off, but it didn't matter. It was fun for all. Felix behaved like he lost twenty years that hour.

During the fishing extravaganza, the seas calmed. Those lost in Spanish class didn't notice the lay down. However, I did. They had enough Spanish mackerel to eat fresh and give a good mess to their

140

friends. It was time for a change. Florida snapper and sea bass would maintain the levity.

A fifteen-minute ride to a large piece of lime rock bottom permitted snack and chatter time. I couldn't make out the entire conversation, but it was nice to overhear the parts I could. They all enjoyed themselves. I couldn't help but smile a moment while running to the reef. Jake rigged up some light bottom outfits in the cockpit as they picnicked on the bow. He, also, trimmed out some belly strips for bait. We were ready when the boat came to rest on anchor.

The Florida snapper mixed with a few sea bass bite made the Spanish event seem slow. Everyone, after a couple of learning lessons, began to roll-up Florida snapper moments after the bait hit the bottom. Jake propped the cooler lid open. Thankfully, Felix, Larry, and Tim started tossing fish in the five gallon buckets we set out and baited their own hooks as needed. Jake and I had our hands full, literally, with the ladies. The fish were additional.

The fun went on until a one-hundred-twenty-quart cooler was slap-full of fish with scattered ice. It took a little over an hour and a half.

Fran said, "That's enough, I'm tired."

The lady Matriarch set the course. We cruised back in with Larry and Linda in one beanbag, Tim and Ann in the other, and Felix and I wedging Fran between us on the captain's bench. They all nodded off, some all the way others part way, during the forty-five minute ride to #1 Steinhatchee. Even Jake took a cushion from an aft bench seat to nap on the deck.

It was a good day for all aboard. During the ride in, I had time to think about everything–the trip and those onboard. The charter was originally supposed to be offshore grouper, red snapper with some amberjack thrown in, and maybe a kingfish or cobia. It didn't work out that way due to sea conditions. Nonetheless, everyone had a good time.

Felix and Fran had been coaxed out of their retirement box by their offspring to try something different. Both of them had had a lifetime of work, parenting, and rote living. They took care of family needs before themselves, neither leaving time for or wanting frills for themselves.

Larry and Linda lived with pressure. Larry worked a high-pressure career. His ideas and decisions carried million-dollar minimums. Linda dealt with him, along with the responsibility of raising their children pretty much alone. And whatever they did outside of home, they both coped with the grind of traffic through the suburbs and the urban metropolitan Atlanta area. A drive to go get anything was best made during periods when the traffic ebbed.

Tim and Ann maintained a slow paced life, rather mundane, in the small town they grew up in. Everybody knows your name, and if you don't keep your mouth shut, everyone will know your business. Tim spent his career amongst some folk he really didn't like being around, but he stuck it out for good money for his family. He kept his mouth shut many times because they couldn't afford for him to lose his job.

Regardless which person, today they each felt something, perhaps escape out of their individual box. It was something different. A valve was opened, releasing pressure that had been building for X too much time. Each one of them became lost in private moments, fighting some silly fish. What they individually felt wasn't the wiggle of a fish, but the loss of stress from the overwhelming reality of life, life uplifted at an individual level.

I was happy to be with them, included, when together they felt the pressure of life hoisted. In my home growing up, my mom had a hand-burnt, wood placard prominently displayed on the kitchen wall that read, "Count no day unimportant if you still have each other, for the day will come when you would give everything for just one day, any ordinary day, you once shared together." It was unsigned. Is that not true? It makes me want to add a few more extraordinary days in my life to fall back on.

If you measure a fishing trip or hunting adventure by the pound of flesh returned, you are a fool. You are missing the real point of time together. The precious importance of sharing life.

Why do people go fishing? Some say they fish to get fish. This is obviously false.
John W. Randolph

Bad Apples

"Look at what else I'm bringing, cuz," Jimmi announced to his buddy Bobby Lee. Then he whipped a handled bottle of whiskey, half full, from behind his back.

"So if we run out of beer, we can keep on rolling," Bobby Lee quipped. He put the bottle on ice in their fish cooler with the frozen shrimp. The boat was then fully loaded.

The jon boat deck was made from thin, untreated plywood rough cut with a jigsaw and flopped on top the aluminum stringers that free slid side to side—not screwed down—with every sway of the boat. A boat that was crumble rotten along the edges. On top of the deck starboard between the middle bench seat and the bow platform was a sun-bleached, crinkled-plastic tackle box that held, stowed inside a handful of jig heads, six plastic bags of jig bodies of various colors and flavors, a variety of hooks of size and condition, a jumble of sinkers that rolled around in the bottom, some used, rust-stained popping corks, three Mirror lures with crusty hooks, two gold spoons colored corrosion blue, three pounds of unidentifiable rusted stuff mixed in here and there, and five roaches—not referring to the insect by the same name. Overtop of the tackle box, spanning the bench seat and the bow platform were four medium-weight, garage-sale, spinning combos. Every one of the poles had at least one eye missing, mostly two, with corroded, spike-pointed fragments still attached. They were handling a soon to be needed tetanus shot.

Forward and port of the middle bench seat, a paper sack with a wet bottom contained a plastic bag of beef jerky, cans of potted meat, beans and wieners, a bag of Tom's hot chips, a generic-brand, gallon-sized, plastic freezer bag filled with homemade boiled peanuts, a two liter bottle of Mountain Dew, and a bottle of Texas Pete hot sauce. A large fish cooler was bungee corded to the front casting deck. It was half full of ice and contained the whiskey and frozen shrimp. On the right of the fish cooler, a five gallon bucket held a twenty-foot section of heavy cord tied to a cinder block. Behind the middle seat was the beer cooler. It was maxed out with beer, and ice was scattered between the cans of suds. A six-gallon gas tank was behind the rear bench seat. An oar, one side splintered off, lay on top of the fuel tank. A modified milk jug for bailing water was in the very back as well. A solid cypress pole, almost the length of the boat, was bungee corded to the port side. On the transom hung a yank start, well used and abused—handed down or *borrowed*—kicker motor. If it had ten horses, they were lame and passed a lot of smoke from their behinds when asked to giddy-up and go. Dabs of JB Weld marked many rivets exposed above the plywood deck. The dabs of weld obviously came after the hand-done, camouflage, spray paint mishap. Andy Warhol might have appreciated the paint job if Andy, Jimmi, and Bobby Lee happened to have been together in a similar state of mind.

The trailer wasn't in as good of shape as the boat. Leaf springs were coupled U-bends of rusted, flakey steel that squeaked when squished down. Bearing grease oozed front and back from both wheels. The tires were almost Kojak bald with one or two bulging cysts on the backside sidewalls. The rubber was the dictionary side photo if you were looking up *dry rot*. The trailer tongue didn't have a jack, rather a thirty-inch section of a four-by-four post strapped down behind the winch to prop up the trailer so the boat could drain rainwater when not in tow. The trailer lights flickered with each bump in the road. The license plate tag expired so many years ago it had flaked off, yet it was immortalized in a rectangle gritty patch of the sticky residue. The trip started with a beer—make that two—and another to cover the ten minute ride.

At the very end of a rough, lime-rock road was an unimproved boat ramp locally referred to as a "put over" towards the head of Sand Gnat Creek. The creek went by as many names as those who fished there, but Sand Gnat seemed most appropriate. The sand gnats were so thick there in the warm mornings and evenings, they taught untold numbers of rednecks to break dance in the backwoods way before young talented black men perfected the moves in the inner cities—and not from a cloud of biting bugs giving crazed instructions.

They shoved the boat off the trailer and simply used the cypress pole to guide the boat along in the outgoing tide. Towards the mouth of the creek, a small tributary dumped in from the south side. There was a deep hole. It was formed by a freshwater spring that was twelve feet deep at the lowest low tide. That secret spot was passed down knowledge to Jimmi and Bobby Lee from relatives who used to net mullet and commercial fish. They had planned on spending low tide anchored on the side of it. If they had a dollar for every fish that came out of that hole over history, they'd still be in that same boat doing what they were doing, but with a lot of money buried around.

On the drift out, they picked up "free fish," four trout and one redfish. When the boat drifted into the hole, they were about an hour early of dead low tide. Jimmi pushed the boat over to the windward bank. It was easier to cast with the wind at their backs. Bobby Lee chunked out the cinder block anchor into the marsh-grass and let out a Rebel yell. They chugged the rest of a beer they were drinking and grabbed another. They didn't fish, opting to "get right" while the tide fell completely out, dead low. Fluid drained from the creek and the beer cans, and eventually the two fellas, at a steady pace. Oyster cups slowly began to grow above water surface in the last of the receding tide, surrounding most of the pool. The tide stopped moving.

Jimmi looked over his right shoulder to Bobby Lee and said, "You ready, spaghetti?"

He shook it off a little, zipped up, and took hold of a fishing pole rigged with just a lead head jig. Bobby Lee tossed him a frozen shrimp. They both hooked a shrimp on the jig and cast it into the spring pool. A double hook up started a fish toss that lasted for over an hour. Bobby Lee opened the cooler lid and took the liquor and bag of shrimp out before the first two fish were tossed in, and he didn't close it until it was full. Then, the beer cooler, which had plenty of room by then, was used for the remaining catch. All the fish went in the two boxes, no measurement, no matter. When the bite stopped, they had two coolers of trout, redfish, sheepshead, and a couple of flounder, and no beer.

They took their good time, passing the bottle back and forth, rinsing it back with the Mountain Dew, all the while crowing about how they were such good fishermen. Bobby Lee about fell out of the boat, dragging the cinder-block anchor through the marsh grass. Jimmi about fell over laughing at Bobby Lee.

They putt-putted back to the put over and managed to get the boat on the trailer. Somehow, both got wet up to the waist in the process.

145

The two-mile ride back to the house required the overtime work of guardian angels.

Parking in the middle of the yard, they stumbled out of the truck and said, "We'll clean the fish in the morning." They wobbled inside the aged, rust-streaked, singlewide trailer they stayed at, took a couple of straight shots from the whiskey bottle and passed out in the living room recliners.

The next morning came after noon, and it wasn't a good one. The sun had been up for over six hours, and it was smoking hot outside. They reeked of sweat, fish, stale beer, liquor, and the same damp clothes they fell in Sand Gnat creek wearing. Cleaning fish wasn't even mentioned. The next day was work; that evening bed came early. The following day they worked but got together to clean the fish under the pole barn. Ice was long gone off the fish. The fish were warm to the touch, looked funny, and smelled funky. Jimmi and Bobby Lee dumped the fish in the woods and finished the whiskey, tossing the empty bottle in the pile of rotting fish.

Two days later, a game warden was led to the fish pile by circling buzzards. Judging by where the fish were dumped, picking up some sign and knowing the people around, he was quick to put one and one together. On their next fishing escapade, Jimmi and Bobby Lee got an unexpected can't afford the fine, must serve the time surprise.

***

That was a funny but sad story, but it happens every day somewhere. It might involve fish or game. There are only a few bad apples, yet those few ruin it for the rest of us. However, I've found the vast majority of fishermen and hunters gladly abide by the rules and regulations. We simply enjoy being a part of the great outdoors. We plan for it, lead our children to it, and go into it whenever life allows.

Nonetheless, we've all got at least a little bad in us; we were born that way. Sometimes it is hard to do the right thing. While taking a ride down some dirt roads relaxing and listening to your favorite tunes, you may notice a buck, with a rack so big you could hang a load of laundry on it, feeding in a clearing. It must be deaf because it doesn't take notice of you. Your bow is behind the truck seat. He is out of season. No one would be the wiser....

146

Or you've been fishing all day offshore managing to put together a mess of Florida snapper but only catching undoubtedly short grouper. Toward the end of the day, you reel up a red grouper, lay it across the measuring stick, squeeze the tail, squeeze it twice more, and it barely misses the mark. You could sneak it....

Once I was flats fishing with my mom and dad. She caught a trout and was so excited about it. Mom loved to fish more than Dad. I laid it across the law-stick. It was just shy.

"Mom we've got to throw this one back. It is too short."

"Too short for what, babe?"

"Too short to keep."

"Says who?"

"It's the law Mom."

"Let's sneak it back in."

Quandary, do I break the law or Momma's heart?

Thankfully, Dad chirped in, and I got to sneak the trout back in the water. In her defense, Mom was raised during the Great Depression in West "by God" Virginia; to her, I was throwing away food. That was sinful; the law was flawed.

There is the other side of the coin that needs to be taken into consideration. The vast majority of young men and women choosing a career in wildlife management do so because they love the outdoors and everything involved. By and large, there is no great money to be made in the career choice. Perhaps they begin thinking others value what they love similarly to the way they do. But after encountering enough "bad apples" with short, extra, or out of season fish, or game stashed away and caught. Those lying and trying to deceive them cause a callousness to develop. Tie that together with when the legal system fails to support their efforts, and they feel disrespected from both ends. They become, understandably, jaded.

The fish and game officers, with just cause, learn to distrust John Q. Public (JQP), you and me, because they encounter the few "bad apples" too frequently. It is easy for them to become unenthusiastic, developing a negative first impression over time.

The chance meetings between game wardens and us, JQP, shouldn't be in an atmosphere of mutual distrust and presumption. The meetings should be friendly, even appreciated. After all, the game warden is just doing his/her job, protecting our resources from the "bad

147

apples." The encounter may involve ticket reminders over safety issues or coming to our rescue some unfortunate day.

Some argue we pay their salary, and they shouldn't annoy us on our day off. I find the salary "we" pay them to be insufficient. How many JQPs require packing a gun as part of our job requirement? I admire "the man." I most admire the officer who approaches with a good attitude.

We, as recreational anglers, charter boats included, outdoorsmen overall, need to be responsible with the resource—a resource we apparently love a lot by the bunch of money we spend to enjoy it.

The vast majority of us straight-up outdoorsmen and outdoorswomen have witnessed or known of others abusing our resource. That includes folks catching a limit of fish in the morning then returning in the afternoon to take another quota. Tell them the way you feel about what they did non-confrontationally, in a friend to friend chat. Sometimes a sincere talk from a good friend can make a big change. If that doesn't do it, drop an anonymous tip.

People who abuse a natural resource don't care about it. Once that particular supply is gone, they move on to rape another. They'll leave you empty to miss what you used to love to do.

We need to exercise personal responsibility; otherwise, the government becomes more involved by regulations and management. And we know their poor management skills can lead to bankrupting a combination whorehouse, liquor, and pawnshop in downtown Las Vegas within a year.

Nature is the art of God.
Dante

The Yearning

Ghost writing - another man's passion

From my accounting office, the taller building across the street blocked the sun from my window before it set. Even though it was summer, the untimely sunset touched me with a winter gloom. After work, when I exited my building, the trapped heat, released from the buildings and streets, let me know in one hot breath, it was summer. Thank God for whoever invented air conditioning.

Thin rectangular shafts of sunlight from the west divided the towering block statues as I waited on the bus, to get to the subway, to my car, and then home. I couldn't wait to escape the concrete jungle.

The longed for three-day weekend was coming in two more days. My family, wife, and two daughters–five and six years old–were going to Steinhatchee for a short vacation.

A couple of our close friends had visited there last year during scallop season. They returned raving about what a great, laid-back time they had. They vacationed at a place called Steinhatchee Landings that had amenities such as a tennis court, petting zoo, etc., and a boat dock. They also referred to Steinhatchee, as a "po-dunk" little Northwest Florida fishing village, saying that during scallop season, the place was flooded with people. If we wanted to go at that time, we needed to make our reservations well in advance, not short notice.

I checked it out via Internet. The Landings had more luxuries than I required, but my wife, Brenda, and the girls would enjoy the amenities. It cost a bit more, but the benefits were worth it, to me, for them. Honestly, the boat dock sold me solid. I made the reservations well ahead of time. I just wanted a family getaway. Scalloping was this year's vacation excuse.

Secretly, I selected a unit with a Jacuzzi in the master bath. With luck, the love of my life would join me after the girls were tucked in. I knew her favorite wine; it would be chilled.

Brenda had been slowly packing for two weeks, which explained why some of our clothes were temporarily unavailable. Those missing clothes, set aside for the trip, were scattered around and on the bed of our guest bedroom. Other miscellaneous packed items ranged from snack foods—enough to feed the entire Girl Scout troop a week, *cute* new clothes for the girls, and, of course, for their mom, new shirts, and shorts for me…just to keep me quiet about their stuff, sun block of various ratings and scents, two new *clean* coolers, a dive flag I was told we had to have while scalloping, and snorkeling gear still in blister packs. On top of one of my small stacks to go was underwear draped over stylish yet modest swim shorts and a small, obvious Victoria's Secret box, taped shut with a handwritten note "confidential." That Pandora's succubus box kept me thinking about what I might uncover during vacation and taped my mouth shut from saying anything stupid about financially recovering after this mini-vacation. Never underestimate the shrewdness of a woman.

Once I noticed my missing clothes and was told where they were stashed, I'd snuck peaks into the guest bedroom at the accumulation of unnecessary, until the night before leaving. I expressed my concerns to Brenda about whether our SUV had space to haul all the "necessary" items plus my bay boat with fishing gear. She informed me that many things were packed in large, plastic-storage containers and would ride in the boat. As long as the Victoria Secret box was rolling safely amongst the rest, I would have rented a U-Haul.

The ride down to Steinhatchee was trouble-free. The lodging and grounds were picturesque. However, I had a nag, a Jones, I needed a fix. I really wanted to go fishing without carrying my beloved "baggage." If it were just Brenda, I could deal with it, but for Brenda to go, it meant the girls as well. I love them all, but that wasn't what I needed. I needed escape fishing. I needed to get outside the shadows.

I told Brenda, in private, about my desire to fish, by myself, two evenings before our trip. She told me it was fine. She'd make a big prolonged breakfast, and then procrastinate with the girls. She's great! But she said it would be best if I went early in the morning and come back by "ten-ish." That seemed perfect for me. We had a deal.

150

Saturday morning I slipped out the door thirty minutes before daylight. The coolers were pre-iced with food and drink, the fishing poles were pre-rigged, and the tackle box trays were in my anal bean-counter order.

The flashlight illuminated idle down river was over eleven months too long. When I saw the sign ending the "No Wake Zone," it yelled what the NASA controller says after saying one. "Blast off!"

Over my left shoulder, the sun backlit the tree line. Some tall isolated palm trees were in silhouette. The sky was soft light, a lot of orange yellow with some pink hues. The smell of saltwater with a hint of burnt two-cycle oil was fine perfume. I was released from indenture, a verse from a Jimmy Buffet song I know, but couldn't remember the title.

The Gulf of Mexico was calm…smooth with undulated rollers, allowing my bay boat to cruise faster than normal. Thirty-two knots with no pounding was a blessing. Not familiar with the area, enjoying the ride, I went westerly, pushing the bow somewhat south. I didn't care if I caught a fish at all; I just needed life-release. I was running the outdoor office I wanted so much to be in more often. I could fart in this office and not worry about it. I did and smiled.

Fifteen minutes into my ride I noticed bait pods dimpling about eleven o'clock off my bow. I turned that way. More bait pods became visible to the left and right, some of which were spraying the surface; evidently fish were feeding on them. That was confirmed when I noticed larger fish leaping from the surface. Most of those arched in and out gracefully, some ungracefully flop landed, and every now and then, I saw one cartwheel. I had found my fantasy on water!

I wondered why no other boats were around to experience what I was witnessing. I was alone amongst a carnival of fish. My hands were trembling while trying to pick one of my three trout poles. One had a jig tied on, the other a small silver spool, and the third a small topwater plug. I had covered the bases with my best lures in advance. What to cast first?

I started with the silver spoon. I landed multiple ladyfish, two bluefish, and one Spanish before the spoon was cut off. I didn't bother to re-tie, simply switched to the top water plug. The fish mobbed the plug upon entry, and it was cut away. I picked up the jig rod with thirty pound leader and proceeded to catch bluefish, ladyfish, and Spanish, as long as I fished the next tormented bait pod.

151

The jig was cut off so many times and the leader was trimmed so far back to the mainline, I had to sew on another section of leader. But instead of tying another jig head to the mono leader, I decided to Haywire twist on a short piece of light #1 wire at the end of the leader to prevent off the cutoffs, and continued with topwater lures. My lure was a "Pup Dog." It was as effective as throwing a cornflake in a commercial catfish pond. I don't think what I tossed mattered. A topwater lure tossed in the bargain bin at "Fish Mart" for a quick hit would have worked just as well. Seeing a fish hit a topwater lure you toss instantly, becomes a forever memory. Listen to any fisherman's tale of tail.

I glanced at my watch and saw the numbers 10:13 am. I was going to be family late! I pushed the engine, boat, and myself, racing so not to be late enough to really upset Brenda. The "No Wake" zone was never-ending to The Landing. I imagined my wife giving me justified grief for being late, but the extra fun would be worth the fuss. The joy of my experience would insure extra funds for us to come back again next year.

Luckily, in some twisted sense, one of my girls required some attention for one of those non-emergency little girl emergencies. One of those "whatever," Mommy I need your attention moments. My tardiness went unnoticed.

I unloaded the boat and rinsed it out. Brenda had stacks of stuff piled together and ready for me to put on the boat. My boat should have been renamed *U S Minnow* because I was packing to go to *Gilligan's Island*. There were two iced coolers. One cooler was full of food and drinks; the other was for the scallops. There was the original plastic shopping bag, now torn, jammed with the snorkel gear still in the blister packs. There was a storage tote with a bulging lid filled with towels and extra clothes for the girls. Two oversized, flowery, beach bags bulged out with snacks, sun blocks, a First Aid box, and other stuff I couldn't see underneath the stuff on top. It took three trips back and forth to get the job done.

I was in a pouring sweat before the girls paraded down accompanied by the popping heel sounds of fresh flip-flops. They had donned floppy sunhats, stylish sunglasses, and new bathing suits under cover-ups and all smelled like a pina colada. Brenda was the one not wearing water wings. After things settled down, we were off to a fine family day of scalloping.

I had no idea what I was doing. The locals had given me some quick advice. It boiled down to, go look for boats bunched together and respectfully raft-up amongst them. That is what I did. I sought the boats and respectfully rafted in amongst them.

By the time I did that, the girls had rifled through every box and bag. The boat looked like the aftermath of Christmas morning. I had to stop three times to keep stuff from blowing out, and we still lost an open bag of chips, but we made it.

It took twenty-five minutes to break into the blister packs of snorkel gear. Whoever developed that packaging design needs to go through life with their thumbs removed. It took thirty minutes to fit the girls with their snorkel equipment. Once we got through the pinched faces and toes and tangled hair, they looked darling. It took ten minutes for our little ducklings to follow mama duck into the water. They rode Brenda like she was a trained dolphin, asking about everything, including how to catch the scallop. A scallop was something they had never seen before in their lives and were sure not to catch today. The water wings insured the scallop's safety.

I cannonballed from the boat, splashing everybody. We spent some time together before I slipped away in search of this illusive scallop. I saw one resting atop the grass below, dove down, and grabbed it. I was so proud of myself. I went over to the girls and showed if off. They gave me the attention I wanted.

Of all the stuff we brought, we forgot the mesh bags to put the scallops in, so I gathered a handful, swam back to the boat, put them in the cooler, and did that re-do for almost an hour before Brenda had had enough of being the mama dolphin.

We all loaded back in the boat, took off the snorkel gear, and toweled off. The two girls wrapped in towels wanted to see my catch of scallops. I picked one up and showed it to them. They were in awe of it for almost a minute before they went back to the "little girl world" of sunhats and sunglasses, fruit drinks, apple slices, etc.

The Marine Patrol slipped up on me. We exchanged greetings. The two men were very polite. They looked at the deck of the boat scattered randomly with swim fins, towels, flip-flops, masks, food, drink bottles half empty, and Brenda with two, young, wild-haired girls who clung to her. The girls stared at them like possessed children from a horror film. I asked if they wanted to see Brenda's and my fishing licenses, fire extinguisher, life jackets, scallops, or anything else.

153

They said, "No, but we did notice you weren't flying your dive flag."

I pointed to it lying in a corner of the boat.

They wrote me a ticket, explaining it was a reminder for the safety of those two, pretty, little girls. One officer told me he had a set himself. I wanted to get mad, but I understood.

We tidied up the boat before running back in. The girls helped off load the boat, once at the dock. I washed the boat. While washing the boat, I was introduced to a small insect locally called a no-see-um. Nobody had bothered to tell me about those biting bugs. If my count was correct, I met one billion and six.

I ended up paying a local lady to shuck our scallops. She laughed when I told her of my attempt, apparently a hammer is not needed to clean a scallop. I blame my rash behavior on those maddening no-see-ums.

We were all beat. A pizza was in order. Brenda got the girls showered while I picked up the pizzas. My baby girls nibbled on a slice or two. They were so tired they didn't fight about going to bed. Brenda tucked the sleepyheads in.

I was in the master bath drawing hot water in the Jacuzzi, thinking about how early the girls went to bed, how sound they would sleep and…, the wine! I ran downstairs, pulled it from an extra cooler where it was hidden, passed through the kitchen, snagging two long stem glasses, and was back upstairs without Brenda noticing.

I was in that huge, hot water, jet master tub ten minutes before Brenda walked in. She looked yummy yet tired. The ten minute prelude had taken much of the zip out of my do-da. I could have fallen asleep and drowned before her arrival. She stepped in and eased back across from me with a sigh. She wiggled to get a water jet where she needed it most.

Ten years ago, before the girls, the hot water from the Jacuzzi would have wet the bedding in loving transfer. Tonight we individually washed. I gave her a quick shoulder massage without intention. We'd been married long enough not to be as impetuous as in yester-years.

I toweled off, did my after shower gig, finger-fluffed my hair, and pulled on a pair of boxer briefs, adjourning quickly to the master bedroom. Brenda remained behind me. The firm, king size bed with the tight fitted bottom sheet, crisp top sheet, and designer plump comforter was calling me. That comforter was so comforting I thought about stealing it. I peeled the bottom and top sheets apart and rolled between them, laid back, my head cradled in a feather cloud.

I noticed Brenda over my left shoulder, backlit from the dimmed light shining from the master bath, wearing the sheer "secret" from the box. Her silhouette shined trough the veneer, showing a trim line I wanted to see, honestly, all the time. I caught the scent of her perfume. That aroma brought me back to when we first tackled each other.

I knew the "mama dolphin" was tired, yet she was willing to love me through her exhaustion. I fell deeper in love with her for her devotion.

It wasn't the moment. We were both exhausted. We cuddled. I told her about my morning, a time I had longed for and enjoyed so much. We talked about the girls, how cute they looked, and shared a few laughs about some of their comments or behaviors, including the meltdown moments and the happy. It was so wonderful. I told her she was hot in the nighty, and then whispered in my lover and best friend's ear, "I'll shuck that in the morning."

Brenda responded, "What did you say?"

She thinking I said something dirty. I didn't but kind of yearned it that way.

Thanksgiving invites God to bestow a second benefit.
Robert Herrick

Eavesdropping

I spend many an hour on the boat passively eavesdropping via the VHF radio on channel 9. It is similar to piped in music while riding an elevator, but it is talk radio. Floating in the vastness of the Gulf of Mexico and hearing another person's voice greater than a boat length away can give a sense of comfort in case something goes terribly wrong on my boat or theirs. Mostly, what I hear is idle chitchat with a country-fried trucker overtone. However, a VHF—Very High Frequency—ship to shore radio is completely different than a CB—Citizens Band—radio used along the roadways with drivers using numeric codes. I'm listening in like I'm rolling a big rig down I-95 with a load of moving marine parts, fishing accessories, and fresh-iced fish.

On weekends, the radio waves are so constipated a ten minute silence can give necessary solitary relief. The weekend verbal radio diarrhea has squeezed charter captains into switching channels to eliminate over hearing poop-by-poop successes and false alarm fish stories from other floating thrones.

Surprisingly, one thing the radio does is indiscreetly transmit information to all listening about how well the favored offshore fish, grouper, are biting. If the bite is on, it is a wonder some fishermen actually spend enough time to reel in a fish before grabbing the microphone to tell their buddy and everybody else about it.

"What about it Rubber Ducky, this is Daddy's Paycheck.

"Go ahead; you got the Rubber Ducky."

"We're killing 'em."

"Where ya at?"

"You remember that place we were at a few weeks ago with Uncle Chewy?"

"Yea. You bottom fishing?"

"Trolling."

"What are you fishing with?"

"You remember that plug I bought at the Walmart when we were there with the girls…? Green and yellow with the black stripes?"

A long silence follows because Daddy's Paycheck failed and broke Fishing Man Code #69.DA1 a.k.a. letting the cat out of bag.

After an uncomfortable delay, "Teeeeeen fo'."

I wonder what Rubber Ducky said to himself after he let go of the microphone?

Someone spitting glee over the radio about catching fish is fine if everyone is doing equally well. However, the radio guy who discovered a hotbed of fish and can't keep himself off the radiophone can be as unwelcome as discovering a wasp nest in the electronic box, if you're not catching fish.

"How 'bout it Stink Bait. This is Mamma's Wedding Ring."

"Go ahead."

"How ya doing?"

"We're picking up some grunts, 'bout it."

"One more grouper and I'm limited out!"

"Ten four. That is great," un-clicking the radio mic and saying where he wanted him to stick Mamma's Wedding Ring.

The words of one gleeful angler wafts across the radio waves of less fortunate boats like a fart in church when no one says anything aloud, but we all want to get up and leave the pew.

I've had days when we were picking up a fish here and there. A slow process of making a good basket of fish can put a drag on the day.

Then Bubba chirps in, "How 'bout it Reef Robber; this is Wave Whacker."

"Go ahead. You got R&R."

"How ya doing?"

"We 'bout to wrap this up, one more, you?"

"We limited, headed to the hill."

"Teeeen fo'; we'll be right behind you."

It takes much self-restraint not to grab the mic and yell, "Shut up! I'm trying to make a living out here!"

Instead of doing that, I use it as an incentive to fish harder. I've also learned not to let it get to me. The next day, when no one who was on my boat the previous day could find out the whole truth, and presuming we were less successful than Reef Robber and Wave

157

Whacker, of course, I find out those two boats limited out with ten grouper each. By passively eavesdropping, they had me somewhat concerned I was doing less than a good job. They threw a disappointing atmosphere via the radio on us with our less than limit of twenty-four. It sounded like we weren't doing as well, but in fact, we were doing just fine.

"How 'bout it Fishing Fool? This is Bone Shaker."

"Go ahead."

"You ain't going to believe this, but we got nine hawg grouper. The smallest is fifteen pounds, and the biggest is close to thirty."

"Way to go 'hawg dawg!' Got pictures?"

"Naw, but I'm going to get one of those idiot proof cameras at the marina when we get back to the dock."

"Teeeen fo'."

I listened to that and turned to see five guys looking at me. The largest grouper we had might've pushed just over ten pounds.

A while later, one asked, "Captain, what's the biggest grouper you ever caught?"

I smiled and said, "thirty-one pounds." Then I got to tell the truth. "Twenty five and half on the scales…good for our neck-of-the-Gulf."

I tried to explain, "Radio fish can weigh a bunch more than land fish."

I erased some of the confused looks when I continued, "A radio fish can lose fifty percent of its weight when pulled out of the cooler at the marina."

The rest of the confusion was lifted when I related that I remember, after a charter, asking a fellow I knew how he did while fishing that day. He told me he caught a thirty-five pound grouper. I said I'd never seen a thirty-five pound grouper come off a recreational boat in Steinhatchee. I asked where it was at, and he replied, "In my cooler on the boat."

"That is a whale of a catch; I'd like to see it if you don't mind."

He was proud to show me, but by the time he slid off the Tiki barstool and faltered to his boat, the fish had verbally lost ten pounds. It lost five more pounds after he stepped on the boat. It lost a couple more pounds once the cooler lid came open. It was a fine eighteen-pound gag grouper. The point is: Don't believe everything you hear or are told.

The radio can get hushed when the favored offshore fish, grouper aren't cooperative. It's been quiet lately during the heat of summer.

Keeper grouper are hard to come by inside of sixty-five feet—thirty to thirty-five nautical miles off Steinhatchee, Florida—when the sky-heater is set on broil. The Gulf waters are dreadfully calm, the air thick, hot, and moist. Salt vapor, and the still heat can make time crawl.

Toward the end of the day, some will quip that the fishing was terrible. "We wasted the day to catch two or three grouper."

And I think, *No you wasted a day because you chose to grouper fish all day.* They're other fish in the sea. Many of which are so active that you must have seen them vault themselves out of the water to show you.

"Oh, those are just jack crevalle, Bonita, Spanish mackerel, bluefish, or barracuda; I don't like eating those!"

"When's the last time you missed a meal?"

Would it be a horrible waste of time to take an hour to toss a spoon, plug, or anything into a school of exploding fish and have your reel drag heat up hotter than your temper at not catching fish? Heck, scare yourself, and use the lightest tackle to test yourself. If you lose the fight, what have you lost? Watch out! That inedible, waste-of-time fish just slapped a smile on your face and made you stop thinking about how hot it was. It gave the rest of the crew something fun to do besides sweat excessively because you're obsessed with a single species of fish. Goodness, it's a win, win and win Triple Crown of fishing fun.

One week I had a fourteen-year-old boy land a barracuda six inches shorter than he was tall. That day we caught a good number of grouper and some red snapper. But what fish do you think he's talking about when he tells his friends at school about his weekend fishing trip? Don't fish with your stomach. Life offers too few fishing trips to get anchored down by what you pass through your gastrointestinal tract. Fish with your mind, and fill it with great memories.

Sometimes I believe the radio is on the comedy channel. I'll share these two gems.

"Jim, Jim, this is Bob."

"Go ahead, Bob."

"Jim, Jim this is Bob."

"Bob this Jim; what can I do for you?"

"Jim, turn the volume up on your radio. I can barely hear you."

That is the equivalent of turning up the volume on your hearing aid so your wife will pay better attention.

"Mike, Mike, this is Johnny. Mike, Mike this is Johnny. Mike,

Mike this is Johnny!"

This transmission was repeated within the minute for over ten minutes and then... "Mike, turn your radio on."

I have no appropriate commentary; it writes itself. The mate, two others onboard, and I overheard it.

One of the guests said, "Did I just hear that man say...?"

"Yes, I've got to write that down."

And in closing, I hear this ending many VHF transmissions. I suppose it is FAQ, "Ten-four."

The answer is fourteen. Ten plus four equals fourteen. Roger? Oh, just an FYI moment: When you make a statement on your VHF radio and end it with the word *over*, it means you are expecting a reply. When you make a statement on your VHF radio and end it with the word *out*, it means you are not expecting a reply. When you make a statement on your VHF radio and end it with "over and out," it must mean you expect more communication but you don't intend to listen to it. I believe it is analogous to when you're bickering with your other half and she provokes your response, but she ain't going to listen to a word you say. Don't use "over and out." You may have heard it used in old war movies, but it didn't make sense then either.

There is nothing that attracts human nature more powerfully than the sport of tempting the unknown with a fishing line.
Henry Van Dyke

Probability Near Zero

The weather was of fairytale conditions, endless Carolina-blue sky defined loosely by high wisps of cloud streaks going nowhere. The sea was a mirror that erased the horizon. The water and firmament blended seamlessly in the distance—a serenity that doesn't happen often.

Jimmy, Tom, Ricky, Phil, Don, Pete, Jake (first mate), Amber (his best mate), and I were blessed with such a day. It was as good as it can get and, unbeknownst to us, would only get better till the end.

It started with catching pinfish and pigfish on Nine Mile Bank. While en route, several schools of bait cracked the mirrored surface. Predators weren't terrorizing them, so I slid by without stopping. On the south side of the bank was a mosaic of sand holes and grass beds three to six foot deep. The water was gin clear. One could look overboard and see individual blades of grass, shells, and, of course, fish. It was a twenty-minute boat ride to *See World*.

I wanted sixty live bait in the tank before going offshore. Using an eighth-ounce bell sinker, a bream hook, and a pinch of Gulp for bait, the crew loaded the tank and managed to catch a couple of short trout quickly.

The next stop was a halfway point. I try not to go more than forty-five minutes without taking a shot at fish. This time we were going to take a twenty-minute warm-up on Florida snapper, AKA, the ubiquitous pink mouth grunt. On light tackle, Florida snapper was fun-action fishing.

Most of the time, it is difficult to get folks to stop fishing and move on. The "just one more" can last for six more per person or fifteen more minutes, which really doesn't matter. I'd already allowed time for that game.

The sea was in better condition than a new piece of interstate on a dry spring day so I decided to take advantage and cruise to a distant grouper hole. With the lack of wind and the slack tide, we had to anchor twice before setting the boat on top of a small piece of reef. The second anchoring paid off. We lucked up on six, nice gag grouper and a good plenty of short, red grouper before the red snapper chimed in. We tossed back five or six red snapper between seven and nine pounds.

That is hard to do. I do not understand or agree with the red snapper regulations but abide under the thumb of Big Brother. I could rant, but it doesn't do any good; besides I don't want to be a bummer.

With the seas remaining flat, I decided to run to the most distant waypoint and fish our way back to Steinhatchee. Along the way, a single flying fish would squirt from the surface or a covey and blast away from the boat. Some of the newborn fliers were just a few inches long. They were cute, fun to watch, and had significance to be revealed later.

The waypoint I named ET2, should be renamed "Ibuprofen" because that is what you need when it's finished with you. Commercial grade, "reef-donkey" amberjack guard that sweet piece of bottom, and every other brand of fish resides there as well.

***

"Jake, check the drags; it's donkey time," I said as he pulled down the rods while I slowed down.

Anchoring conditions were difficult. Translation: we had to do it twice before it was nice. The second time we anchored spot on. Then nice was, to me, translated as making grown men grunt. Grunt they did as grade A amberjack tried their best to dislocate everything from the hook on back to the lower lumbar. When Amber reeled in a quality amberjack without much-a-do, it knocked the macho down a few notches. Especially since she was considerably smaller than all the men, and she did it on light-weight tackle, thirty-pound test, and was noticeably pregnant. Women are awesome! I did ask her if she wanted my help.

She said, "No," politely.

Ibuprofen gave us exhaustion, a limit of amberjacks, a few nice gags, one red grouper, and one jumbo "mango" snapper. It was time to drift around the hard bottom patches in search of red grouper.

Drift fishing takes away the detail and work of tossing and retrieving the anchor. The dual hull of the Twin Vee allows the boat to drift perpendicular to sea, reducing line tangles. Drift fishing also lets one find new bottom, or at least you find out something about the bottom configuration. Anyway, bopping around, from one piece to the next for an hour or so, put together a limit of red grouper, two of which went into the truck red category. The limit came at the right time. It was time to take the ride back to River Haven Marina in Steinhatchee.

Most were on the bow enjoying a cold drink. Amber was propped up beside me on the captain's bench, enjoying the shade and breeze when one of the guys seated in front of the console started motioning to turn to port. He and I noticed the same thing at the same time, a twig sticking up out of the water. I veered off and turned back. It turned out to be a twelve-foot hickory branch draped in Sargasso weed.

"There might be some dolphin under that," I told Jake. He was already pulling out two light spinning rods. In hindsight, we should have rigged all the light spinning rods before approaching, something to remember.

Before getting within casting range, the guys on the bow got a clear view of the moving neon.

"Dolphin!"

The first cast launched a psychedelic dream that kicked off the freak show. A second break-dancer was hooked up before boating the first fish, good dolphin fishing protocol. Two more rods were put in action, baited with whole threadfin herring. Chaos was in high gear, but during that time, we somehow developed a new procedure called the "dip and dump." It was kind of a NASCAR teamwork approach, where the man with the net dipped the fish for the angler then dumped it on the deck and moved on to the next fish. A dolphin wrangler or two de-hooked the wild fish—a goat roping or greased pig chase have more graceful moments—and attempted to put it in a cooler. The angler was re-baited and put back on track.

The action stopped after the seventh fish. The fish were cookie-cutter three footers, which was a good size for this section of the Gulf of Mexico. They were some of the largest I've seen in Steinhatchee.

What a way to finish the day! The boat was trashed, the way it should look at the end of a good day of fishing. On the ride back in, I had time to reflect. I knew dolphin held to flotsam like that tree limb, but what brought them in? A covey of baby flying fish lit from the surface after that thought. What were the odds of running across a small hickory branch in the middle of nowhere? To the best of my ciphering, the probability was zero, but sometimes it is better to be lucky than good.

Nature is always hinting at us.
Robert Frost

The Joy of Fishing

My lack luster catches were not due to lack of effort or the want to save money on gas, or not trying here, there, and everywhere with this bait or the other. For a while, even the ubiquitous Florida snapper— grunts—weren't overly cooperative. I was feeling like *Forrest Gump* pre-hurricane. I was working harder than ever to bring what fish I could to the dock. Fortunately, the misfortune was being shared amongst the other charter boat captains.

But it still hurt, because I care. I want to exceed expectations, not disappoint people. There is joy in persuading folk to try something new and making them successful at it. There is more fun in the world of fishing than simply dumping meat to the bottom and waiting for a jerk to occur at one end of the line, followed by a return action of the Jerk at the other end. But things hadn't been happening the way I wanted in quite some time, and fishing was becoming something I had to do, not what I desired to do. I needed a break. I was at a low.

Charles Lowe phoned me. He is my "brother from another mother."

"Me, Curtis, and Evan are coming down for your next available day during the week!"

"Charles, I've got to be honest. The fishing ain't that good."

"I don't care if we don't catch a fish; we're coming down."

"The grouper bite hasn't been...."

"I'd be just as happy catching grunts or anything. Don't worry about the grouper. Let's just go have some fun."

"I think we can do that," I mustered, wondering if I could shake off my bad funk and actually have fun.

Charles loves the outdoors. Fishing or hunting is merely an excuse to be where he hankers to be. After a strong storm, I believe you could find the man standing ankle deep on the curb of a flooded parking lot casting a Pop R to parallel yellow stripes. You might hear him walk away muttering, "After the next storm, those yellow stripers might just bite."

He isn't that crazy, but after approximately fifty years of fishing, he has come to appreciate every aspect of it—not just the catching part. His brother, Curtis, is likewise a fishing enthusiast who would attempt to pull a redfish out of an oyster bar choked creek, using sewing thread for fishing line, just to see the strike and have that brief moment hemmed in his mind. Evan, his young, teenage son, doesn't stand a chance of normal development. He'll be a product of his environment. He may turn out to be an American version of Australia's Steve Irwin in the world of fishing, handling crazed toothy fish most sensible folk avoid by cutting the line because they value their life.

The three came down with a truck bed full of fishing sticks of various sizes and a couple of tackle boxes of dreams to come. We set out just wanting enough fish for dinner that night. I planned to dig for grouper in forty-five feet of water with lots of live bait and some frozen bait as backup. I caught a few nice grouper in that area the week before. The grouper gig didn't pan out. After the third no hit wonder hole, Charles switched to a grunt outfit and proceeded to entice the rest of us to join in the action. Collectively we put together a couple of five gallon buckets full—sixty pounds—of those delightfully, delicious, Prides-of-Steinhatchee. Dinner was taken care of, and it was fun doing it. On light tackle, a big grunt puts up a quality fight. We met our grunt dinner quota.

I said, "I know this sounds crazy, but...I've seen Bonita and Spanish mackerel crashing the bait pods on the ride home over the past couple of weeks. How about doing some light tackle fun-n-gun?"

They were all for it. They asked what to rig up with. I suggested small, flashy jigs or silver spoons with a one-foot section of #1 wire leader for protection against the mackerel teeth. They knew how to do it, rigged en route and ready on arrival.

Small hordes of Spanish mackerel were breaking up the first pods of glass minnows we came to. The mackerel were selectively feeding. In other words, if it wasn't a glass minnow, they didn't want it. We spent an hour bouncing from one pod to the next, tediously and endlessly trying to find a glass minnow mimic in our tackle boxes of tricks. It was fruitless. Apparently, a glass minnow is a hard critter to fake.

166

Then the Bonita came in. The difference in hearing "Spanish" verses Bonita feeding is similar to hearing ice being put in a glass verses ice being put through a blender.

Fish weren't just zipping in and out of the minnows, occasionally taking flight. The water frothed on top like when beating egg whites for a long time with the blender on high. The fish knocked each other around, both below and above the waterline, actually bouncing off one another in mid-air. A blind man could find the schools by the sound of the splashing fish and the screeching gulls. Anything tossed into the froth didn't make it out.

We were all using ten-pound test, except for Curtis the four-pound test pilot. When we'd get a Bonita on, which was seconds after the lure hit the water, the drag would shriek. Line would burn off the reels at a rate and duration that caused you to swear something would give way or melt down. It took at least fifteen minutes to bring each six to ten pound fish to the boat. For Curtis, it sometimes took twenty minutes or more.

Multiple hooks were the norm, sometimes requiring us to do the "May Pole" gig to keep the lines straight. It was an exhausting, lovely pandemonium. Our forearms throbbed after too many hook-ups, yet we would do it all over again next chance.

I was going to turn us around back to the feeding fish after Captain Four-pound-test Curtis landed his forever-fought Bonita.

"Hey ya'll look at that!" I said before starting the motors. There was a squall line of wild Bonita, at least a quarter mile long, coming at us, sounding like a train of rain.

"Let's go get us some of that," said Curtis. And we did.

Charles, somehow, caught a huge blue runner amongst the Bonita. I grabbed it and free lined it off the windward side using a 4/0 grouper outfit. It was a "what the heck" bait. I put the clicker on. In less than three minutes, the clicker buzzed. I grabbed the doubled over pole just as a six-foot shark came completely out of the water, marlin style. I don't think it was a bull shark. The line was cut instantly. Sharks were trailing and feeding on the blitzing Bonita. The sharks were like rednecks, myself included, tracking the smoke scent from a slow-rolling BBQ trailer cooking en route.

"Did you see that?" I asked Charles.

Judging by Charles' face and his trimming up a whole ladyfish for bait, he was well aware of what just happened and intended to catch it.

167

I handed him an extra 4/0 combo to attach the ladyfish to. The rig had no wire leader. He tossed it out the back.

Evan and Curtis were both battling Bonita and loving every moment. I joined in the fun. It was amazing how far and how fast the fish would runoff once hooked. We would fight them back in only for another runoff to happen again, again, and again, until it became ridiculous. When I finally got my fish in, I took a break. I was having fun, fishing...real fun. I liked catching some fish, and I enjoyed watching Curtis artfully deal with a rambunctious fish on the sewing thread he called monofilament. I also enjoyed watching young Evan get caught up in the fever. Charles impressed me, knowing he had caught all kinds and sizes of fish in his lifetime, and yet, he could fully enjoy himself fishing for, as he put it, "anything." The only pressure I felt was in my left forearm, given to me by fish most people care little or nothing about catching. Many people consider Bonita a "trash fish," because they're not favored table fare. I don't fish with my stomach, and God don't make trash.

Charles was holding his grouper pole intently.

"What's going on?" I asked.

"I've been getting a bite," he replied.

"I better check my bait," he said.

We could see the tattered ladyfish coming up through the water as he reeled it in. As it neared the surface, an eight-foot hammerhead shark came after it. It boiled away a foot or so from the boat. It was so close I stepped back.

"Oh my!" I blurted.

"What was it? What was it?" Curtis questioned, while fighting Bonita number umpteen.

Charles and I were explaining as Charles let the bait back down. I was hurriedly twisting a wire leader out of #9 wire and cutting a Bonita in half. I literally tossed my half Bonita bait in the water by hand. I was hoping—

"He's after it," Charles said, referring to his bait.

In a second, he struck. The thick grouper pole arched under the strain, and line peeled off a firm drag.

"Evan! Put on a fighting belt and come here son," Charles demanded. I reeled in my gear, took off the half Bonita, tossed it overboard, and stowed away the gear neat.

Evan is thin, faint of weight compared to the rest of us...shall we say, plus-sized gentlemen. The transfer of the pole came with a hard jerking and yanking action.

"Keep him in the boat!"

Charles was right there beside his son. I cleared the clutter from the front of the boat.

Curtis was wrapped up in the final, eternal, battle minutes with his Bonita number umpteen and one. I couldn't adjust the boat toward Evan's favor until Curtis was finished. The shark might pull Evan all the way around the boat in the meantime. Finally, when Curtis got his fish, I turned the motors on, kicking the boat around to keep Evan's fight off the stern quarters.

Evan pumped and grinded to gain a few yards of line, only to have more line pull off to his chagrin. Curtis came in, taking over the coaching business for his nephew. His advice was straight track helpful for wiry Evan under duress. But lean doesn't mean weak.

It was after seven in the evening. The sun was quickly falling out of the sky. The backdrop was lit beautifully, but darkness would soon be upon us. I called out to any VHF radio listener in Steinhatchee. "Mule Kicker" responded. I told him the situation and asked if he could call my wife to let her know we were fine but would more than likely be in after dark. He was happy to punch the numbers I gave him, making the necessary phone call. I was happy he was standing by his radio.

Evan was holding up well after the first fifteen minutes, but he was under a constant heavy load. Another ten minutes passed. The shark cruised close, just under the surface from starboard to port stern, tilting its hammer at us. It was as if the eight foot hammerhead was checking out what he was fighting. The shark dove, taking line at will. The rod shuttered up and down violently in the next minute. Evan stumbled backwards when the taut line parted. Without a steel leader, the fight lasted longer than we all expected. Evan had fought his largest shark and fought it ever so well.

It was a twenty minute ride to the first channel marker. We relived the fight play by play in panel discussion, each recalling something the other or others didn't catch. We made the river in the last glimmer of light. We all did the clean-up-the-boat details, unloaded the equipment, and finished cleaning fish around nine o'clock. It was decided the fish fry was best suited for the next evening.

"How was your day?" asked Gina, my wife, when I got home.

169

I responded, "I found what I didn't know I was looking for, a renewed joy of fishing."

The contentment which fills the mind of the angler at the close of his day's sport is one of the chiefest charms of his life.
William Cowper Prime

Had Some Fun

Little Davy was chalked between Poot and I on the ride back to Steinhatchee. He was leaned against his mamma for the first half of the ride. His hard lean became uncomfortable to Poot in time. Soon, she and I readjusted him, en route, putting his head on her lap and legs across mine, without waking him. He was as done or overdone as anything left on high in a crock pot over the same amount of time, eight-hours.

***

We started the day by hook and lining pinfish and any other baitfish, over a deep, sand-hole pocked grass flat. The water was clear top to bottom, such that we could see hand-sized fish dart-dance quickly in, then out across the sand holes. We could catch glimpses of baitfish pecking at the bait on the hair hooks. After twenty minutes of Davy reeling up the pinfish and such with enjoyment, I whispered to David and tossed out a fish carcass I had grabbed from the bin at the marina fish-cleaning station that morning to inspire baitfish collection.

David lifted Davy up on the gunnel and said, "Watch the dead fish."

The current was so light the boat and carcass separated slowly. The carcass was visibly overrun with a swarm of pinfish, pigfish, spot-tail pinfish, squirrel fish, a few small catfish, and one shark so small the other feeding fish didn't pay it attention. The carcass came to rest on the edge of the sand hole. It was a looting of flesh from leftover bones.

"Wow, Daddy, look at all the fish; let's stay here and fish."

David set him down. Davy rolled up ten more bait quickly. Poot had added a couple dozen unannounced baitfish toward the cause herself. By then, we had enough live bait to cover the day.

"Davy, it is time to go fishing."

"I thought we were Mister Captain."

I talked him into going for something a little bigger, Florida snapper, grunt fishing. Grunts bang baits so fast, I refer to it as yo-yo fishing. The bait hits the bottom, then count to five, set the hook, and reel up a one to three-pound Florida snapper. It would be a fast, ever-continuing "Happy Meal" for Davy.

Davy grunted through the math long enough to supply the fish box with a gracious plenty of Florida snapper and to raise his ego. David and Poot helped inflate both. Garrett happily volunteered to be the little fish noble's butler, taking care of the non-aristocratic details of de-hooking fish, re-baiting, and taking care of the royal game, while keeping the master fully engaged in the quest.

After a good plenty of Florida snapper, I soft-talked to David, "Ya'll got around a hundred pounds of grunts. How much do you want?"

He told me that was more than enough. "What can we do next?"

I sprinted to a close amberjack hole and anchored appropriately. Garrett free-line released two live baits into a bad neighborhood, using 4/0 grouper combos. Just after Garrett set out the second bait, the first pole bucked down.

David forgot about the pressure of being an electrical engineer in Hotlanta when he felt the pressure of a wild fish trying its best to get off the line. Garrett and I played vaudeville fools, sliding in professional solid fishing advice during the struggle. Our silly routine ended with Garrett gaffing a twenty-five pound amberjack aboard.

David was proud happy. Davy was in a state of amazement. Poot had backpedaled time a few years to go into cheerleader mode during the hype. It was celebration time. Hugs, fist-bumps, high-fives, and many photos were taken and then repeated twice more to fill the limit.

It went a couple or more rounds for the fun of it. David cuddled his son Davy for two fun episodes. The fish went back. It didn't matter. Davy caught big fish with his dad.

On the way back to Steinhatchee, I swung by some patchy rock bottom to best troll two, deep-diving plugs. We picked up two gag grouper and one snake kingfish. That rounded out the day.

***

I idled down at the "No Wake" sign with the sun falling still a hand width or a bit more above the horizon. The shift in motor noise didn't alter Davy's sleep state. He remained a small, slumbering log spanning Poot and I on the captain's bench. I made the adjustments to slip the boat as quietly into the slip as an old mule returning to her stall.

Poot woke up Davy. He came to hazily. The first thing he did was stumble toward the fish box. Garrett opened it for him. "Wow. I caught all that?"

Hearing him say that, I smiled greater than Davy.

I went around, bent over a bit and asked, "What do you think?"

Davy responded, "I had fun like you said."

I grabbed him up and squeezed him through his fishing vest.

Held close to my ear he said, "I love you Mister Captain." My eyes watered—my best tip.

The best things in life are free. Praise the Lord!
Salty Dog

www.ingramcontent.com/pod-product-compliance
Lightning Source LLC
Chambersburg PA
CBHW020615250626
47154CB00004B/1523